In the
TWINKLING
OF · AN · EYE

Sydney Watson

SPIRE BOOKS

FLEMING H. REVELL COMPANY
OLD TAPPAN, NEW JERSEY

PUBLISHER'S NOTE

M ULTITUDES in all parts of the world have expressed their approval of this imaginative, yet true-to-Scripture account of what will transpire on this earth at the coming of the Lord. It is written in a style so fascinating that young and old will read it with almost breathless interest from start to finish.

Already many thousands who would never have studied their Bibles, or looked at an ordinary book or pamphlet to learn the precious truth of the Second Coming of the Lord, have been awakened, quickened and even converted by reading "In The Twinkling of An Eye."

Convincingly true, terrible and beautiful in turn, this book is one of the most startling in the annals of Christian literature—just the book to solemnize and awaken careless, ill-taught, professing Christians to a complete realization of the fact that the coming of the Lord draweth nigh.

AUTHOR'S FOREWORD

SOME years ago I received from an important Southern town, a letter from a Ladies' Temperance Committee, to this effect:—"Sir, We the undersigned, are a committee of Ladies, who, for many years, have purchased your "Stories for the People" in very large numbers, for free distribution and loan; always assuming that you were to be thoroughly relied upon as an upholder of strict Total-abstinence principles. But your latest story has sadly undeceived us, as regards your usefulness as a worker in the great cause we are pledged to uphold and further. On *pp——* of your last story, you make your hero, returning from a day's run with the hounds, come upon a woman lying in a lonely place, who has been injured in a trap accident. You say, speaking of your hero's prompt help to the woman, that "taking his hunting flask from his pocket, he forced a few drops of the brandy between the woman's lips, etc." Now, sir, we contend that had you had the cause of Total-abstinence fully at heart, you would have made that huntsman's flask to have contained *water*."

So much for the letter. The moral of it lies on the surface. There are some persons who seem unable to see anything from the side of *real, actual* life—that Ladies' committee could not —whose vision is narrowed down to the tiny slit of their own cramped, cabined life and thought, they have no true *out*look upon life, as a whole.

I preface this foreward with the above incident, because I am perfectly certain that the standpoint from which I have written this book will be utterly, absolutely misunderstood by many earnest loving-hearted people, whose eyes, with my own, have caught the *up*ward gaze "from whence we look for the return of the Lord Jesus Christ."

I would at once acknowledge that the inceptive idea of writing such a book as this was born within me from reading "Long Odds," that wondrous little half-penny booklet written by the late General Robertson, I believe, a booklet that has been so marvellously "owned and blessed."

For five or six years the idea for this present volume has been simmering and seething in my mind. The first and only real problem I had to face in the matter was that of the *principle* involved in using the fictional form to clothe so sacred a subject (for, to me, the near Return of our Lord is the *most* sacred of all subjects.) But the problem of the *principle* was speedily settled, as I remembered how wondrously God had owned and blessed "Long Odds," in which the fictional is the vehicle of the teaching.

Then, too, there are, I know, myriads of people into whose hands "Long Odds," could never, by any chance, fall—for there are multitudes who will not so much as glance at, or touch a tract, while a volume will easily win its way among all classes. There is an enormous percentage of attendants at our churches and chapels, and many otherwise very earnest Christian workers, to whom the whole subject of the Lord's Second Coming is an absolutely unknown realm of Truth—and these I would fain reach and arouse with the message of this book.

To those Christians who are looking for the Return of the Lord, to whom the subject is the most tenderly sacred of all subjects, who will at first sight condemn the use of the fictional element, the dramatic colour in this book—and many good people will, I am assured—I would say, first, that the book is not written for them, and second, that, our Lord Himself, speaking of His own Return, used two very remarkable illustrations from life's strangest dramas. First, *"As it was in the days of Noah, even so shall it be also in the days of the Son of Man. They ate, they drank, they married, they were given in marriage, until* THE DAY, *etc."* Now, think what a myriad *dramas* were being enacted when the flood came. And had the disciples asked their Lord, privately, after His utterance, to explain more fully what He meant, what thrilling stories He *could,* He *doubtless* WOULD *have sketched.* If any Christian cavils at the dramatic in this book, I would refer him or her to Christ's own pointing in

AUTHOR'S FOREWORD.

the picture of Noah's time, then bid them fill out, by help of the feeblest, simplest imagination, the picture of the myriad dramas that were being enacted when that flood came, of old time. Then, if the objector is honest, and is *capable* of the least imagination, he will say "I see! and, now that I see this fact, my wonder is *not* that there is a certain dramatic freedom in this book, but that the writer has kept so powerful a restraint upon his pen."

Again, Christ said:—"*As it was in the days of* LOT," etc. Now think over *this* saying of our Lord's, and remembering what is actually recorded in Genesis, of the *vice* and *crime* of Sodom, (and how, alas! even when saved from the doomed city, Lot and his daughters brought away much of the vicious, criminal essence of the place with them,) think how the Return of our Lord, presently, will mean the snatching away of many of His own out of scenes infinitely more awful than anything I have used herein, or ever hinted at. A book written on the subject here chosen, and written in the vein our Lord Himself suggests in the two passages referred to above, could not have been written in any other way—to be true to life, and to the subject.

Should any reader object to the expository lectures of Major H———, as the chief vehicle for the doctrinal teaching, I would say that personal experience has proved the style to be infinitely more acceptable to readers than that of the dialogue mode.

I have purposely placed special emphasis on the Jewish side of the subject, since the Jewish question is infinitely more closely enwrapped with the fact of our Lord's near return, than many speakers and writers give prominence to.

SYDNEY WATSON.

"THE FIRE," VERNHAM DEAN, HUNGERFORD, BERKS.

CONTENTS

"IN THE TWINKLING OF AN EYE"

CHAPTER I.

TAKEN AT THE FLOOD.

THE man walked aimlessly amid the thronging press. He was moody and stern. His eyes showed his disappointment and perplexity. At times, about his mouth there lurked an almost savage expression. As a rule he stood and walked erect. Only the day before this incident one of a knot of flower-girls in Drury Lane had drawn the attention of her companions to him as he strode briskly along the pavement, and in a rollicking spirit had sung, as he passed her:

> "Stiff, starch, straight as a larch,
> Every inch a soldier;
> Fond o' his country, fond o' his queen,
> An' hawfully fond o' me."

But to-day there is nothing of the soldier in the pose or gait of Tom Hammond.

Yet the time and place ought to have held his attention sufficiently to have kept him alert to outward appearance. It was eleven in the forenoon. The place was Piccadilly. He came abreast of Swan and Edgar's. The pavement was thronged with women on shopping bent. More than one of them shot an admiring glance at him, for he had the face, the head, of a king among men. But he had no eyes for these chance admirers.

Tom Hammond was thirty years of age, a journalist, and an exceptionally clever one, at the time we make his acquaintance. He was a keen, shrewd man, was gifted with a foresight and general prescience that were almost remarkable, and hence was commonly regarded by his journalistic friends as "a coming man." He had strongly-fixed ideas of what a great daily paper should be, but never having seen any attempt that came within leagues of his ideal, he longed—lusted would not be too strong a term—for the time and opportunity when, with practically unlimited capital behind him, and with a perfectly free hand to use it, he could issue his ideal journal.

This morning he seems farther from the goal of his hopes than ever. For two years he had been sub-editor of a London daily that had made for itself a great name —of a sort. There were certain reasons which had prompted him to hope, to expect, the actual editorship before long. But now his house of cards had suddenly tumbled about his ears.

A change had recently taken place in the composition of the syndicate that financed the journal. There were wheels within wheels, the existence of some of which he had never once guessed, and which in their whirling had suddenly produced unexpected results. The editor-in-chief had resigned, and the newly elected editor proved to be a man who had, years before, done him, Tom Hammond, the foulest wrong one journalist can do to another.

Under the present circumstances there had been no honourable course open for Hammond but to resign. That morning he had found his resignation not only accepted, but he found himself practically dismissed.

Enclosed in the letter of acceptance of his resignation was a cheque covering the term of his notice,
together with the intimation that his services would cease
from the time of his receipt of the cheque.

His dejection, at that moment when we meet him,
was caused not so much at finding himself out of employ-
ment as from the consciousness that the new editor-
elect had accomplished this move with a view to his
degradation in the eyes of his profession—in fact, out
of sheer spite.

To escape the crowd that almost blocked the pavement in front of Swan and Edgar's windows, he turned
sharply into the road, and literally ran into the arms of
a young man.

"Tom Hammond!"

"George Carlyon!"

The greeting flew simultaneously from the lips of the
two men. They gripped hands.

"By all that's wonderful!" cried Carlyon, still wringing
his friend's hand. "Do you know, Tom, I am actually up
here in town for one purpose only—to hunt you up."

"To hunt me up!"

"Oh, let's get out of this crush, old man," interrupted
Carlyon.

The pair steered their way through the traffic, crossed
the Circus, stopped for a moment at the beautiful Shaf-
esbury Fountain, then struck across to the Avenue. In
the comparative lull of that walk Carlyon went on:

"Yes, I've run up to town this morning to find you
out and ask you one question: Are you so fixed up—
excuse the Americanism, old boy. I've a dashing little
girl cousin, from the States, staying with my mother,
and—well, you know, old fellow, how it is. Man's an

imitative creature, and all that, and absorbs dialect quicker than anything else under the sun. But what I was going to say was this: are you too fixed up with your present newspaper to forbid your entertaining the thought of a real plum in the journalistic market?"

Hammond's customary alert look returned to his face. He was now "every inch a soldier," as he cried, excitedly, "Don't keep me in suspense, Carlyon; tell me quickly what you mean."

"Let's jump into a gondola, Tom. I can talk better as we ride."

Carlyon had caught the eye of a cab-driver, and the next moment the two friends were being driven along riverwards.

"Someone, some Johnnie or other," began Carlyon, as the two men settled themselves back in the cab, "once called the hansom cab the gondola of London's streets ——"

He caught the quick, impatient movement of Hammond's face, and with a light laugh went on:

"But you're on thorns, old boy, to hear about the journalistic plum. Well, here goes. You once met my uncle, Sir Archibald Carlyon?"

Hammond nodded.

"He is crazy to start a daily," said Carlyon. "It is no new craze with him; he has been itching to do it for years. And now that gold has been discovered on that land of his in Western Australia, and he is likely to be a multi-millionaire—the concessions he has already sold have given him a clear million,—now that he is rich beyond all his dreams, he won't wait another day; he will be a newspaper proprietor. It's a case of that kiddie in the bath, Tom, doncher-know, that's grabbing for the soap—'he won't be happy till he gets it.' "

"He wants to find at once a good journalist, who is also a keen business man; one who will take hold of the whole thing. To the right man he will give a perfectly free hand, will interfere with nothing, but be content simply to finance the affair."

An almost fierce light was burning in the eyes of the eager, listening Hammond. A thousand thoughts rioted through his brain, but he uttered no word; he would not interrupt his friend.

"I told Nunkums last night, when he was bubbling and boiling over with his project, that I had heard you say it was easier to drop a hundred or two hundred thousand pounds over the starting of a new paper than perhaps over any other venture in the world.

"Nunkums just smiled as I spoke, dropped a walnut into his port glass, and said quietly, 'Then I'll drop them.'

"He hooked that walnut out of his wine with the miniature silver boathook—he had the thing made for him for the purpose,—devoured the wine-saturated nut, then smiled back into my face, as he said: 'Yes, Georgie, I am quite prepared to drop my hundred, two hundred, three hundred thousand, if needs be, as I did my walnut. But I am equally hopeful—if I can secure the right man to edit and manage my paper,—that I shall eventually hook out an excellent dividend for my outlay. I want a man who not only knows how to do his own work well, as an editor, but one who has the true instinct in choosing his staff.'

"Of course, Tom, I trotted you out before him. He remembered you, of course, and jumped at the idea of getting you, if you were to be got. The upshot of it is, nothing would satisfy him but that I should come up by an early train this morning—early bird catches the worm, and all that kind of business, you know,—and now, in spite of the fact that my particular worm had wriggled and squirmed miles from his usual habitat, I've caught him. Now, tell me, are you open to treat with Sir Archibald?"

"Yes, and can begin business this very day!" Hammond laughed with the abandon of a boy, as he told, in a few sentences, the story of his dismissal.

"Good!" Carlyon, in his own exuberant glee, slapped his friend's knee.

"Sir Archibald," he went on, "was to come up by the 10:05 from our place, due at Waterloo at 11:49. He'll be fixed up—"Hail Columbia!" again—at the hotel by this time. That's where we are driving to now, and—ah! here we are!"

A moment later the two men were mounting the hotel steps. One of the servants standing in the vestibule recognized Carlyon, and saluted him.

"My uncle arrived, Bates?" Carlyon asked.

"Yes, sir, and a young lady with him!"

Carlyon turned quickly to Hammond.

"That's Madge, my American cousin, Tom. I'm awfully glad she has come; I should like you to know her."

Turning to the servant, he asked, "Same old rooms, Bates?"

"Yes, sir."

Three steps at a time, laughing and talking all the while, Carlyon, ignoring the lift, raced up the staircase, followed more slowly by his friend.

Hammond never wholly forgot the picture of the sitting-room and its occupant, as he entered with Carlyon. The room was a large one, exquisitely furnished, and flooded with a warm, mellow light. A small but cheerful-looking wood fire burned upon the tiled hearth, the atmosphere of the room fragrant with a soft, subtle odour, as though the burning wood were scented. From a couch, as the two men entered, a girl rose briskly, and faced them. She made a picture which Tom never forgot. The warm, mellow light that filled the room seemed to clothe her as she stood to meet them. "America" was stamped upon her and her dress, upon the arrangement of her hair, upon the very droop of her figure. She was tall, fair, with that exquisite colouring and smoothness of complexion that is the product of an unartificial, hygienic life.

Her face could not be pronounced wholly beautiful, but it was a face that was full of life and charm, her eyes being especially arrestive.

"Awfully glad you came up, Madge!" cried Carlyon. "I've run my quarry down, and this is my own particular, Tom Hammond."

He made a couple of mockingly-funny elaborate bows, saying: "Miss Madge Finisterre, of Duchess County, New York. Mr. Tom Hammond, of—oh, shades of Cosmopolitanism!—of everywhere, of London just at present."—Tom bowed to the girl.—She returned his salute, and then held forth her hand in a frank, pleasant way, as she laughingly said, "I have heard so much of Tom Hammond during the last few days, that I guess you seem like an old acquaintance."

Tom shook hands with the maiden, and for a moment or two they chatted as freely and merrily as though they were old acquaintances.

The voice of Carlyon broke into their chat, asking: "Where's Nunkums, Madge?"

Before the girl could reply, the door opened and Sir Archibald entered the room.

One glance into his face would have been sufficient to have told Tom the type of man he had to deal with, even if he had not seen him before. A warm-hearted, unconventional, impulsive man, a perfect gentleman in appearance, but a merry, hail-fellow-well-met man in his dealings with his fellows.

With a bit of mock drama in the gesture, Madge Finisterre flourished her hand towards the newcomer, crying,

"Sir Archibald, George? Lo, he is here!" She flashed a quick glance to the piano as she added, "If only I had known you were about to enter, uncle, I would have treated you to a few crashing bars of stage-life entree-music."

"Go away with your nonsense!" laughed the old man.

"Nonsense, indeed!" the girl laughed as merrily as the old man. Then, with a sudden, swift movement, she crossed to the piano, struck one sharp note upon it, and whispered in well-feigned hoarseness, "Slow music for the three conspirators as they retire to plot the destruction of London's press, and the accumulation of untold millions by their own special journalistic production!"

Her fingers moved over the ivory keys, and low, weird, creepy music filled the room with its eerie notes.

Sir Archibald and George Carlyon fell in with the girl's mood, and crept doorwards on tiptoe.

"Number three," hissed the girl.

And Tom Hammond laughingly followed with the two other men.

"She is a treat, is Madge!" laughed George Carlyon, as the three men passed through the doorway and made for the study-like room of Sir Archibald.

CHAPTER II.

"THE COURIER."

FOR two hours the three men held close conference together. At the end of that time all the preliminaries of the new venture were settled. Tom Hammond had explained his long-cherished views of what the ideal daily paper should be. Sir Archibald was delighted with the scheme, and, in closing with Hammond, gave him a perfectly free hand.

"You were on the point of saying something about a striking poster to announce the coming paper, Mr. Hammond," said the old baronet.

"Yes," Tom replied; "I think a great deal may be done by arresting the attention of the people—those in London especially. My idea for a poster is this: the name of the paper is to be 'The Courier.' Very well, let us have an immense sheet poster, first-class drawing, striking but harmonious colouring, and bold, arrestive title of the paper and announcement of its issue. Following the title, I would have in the extreme left a massive sign-post, a prominent arm of the structure bearing the legend 'To-morrow.' On the extreme right of the picture I would put another signpost, the arm of which should bear the words 'The Day After To-morrow.' I would have a splendidly-drawn mounted courier, the horse galloping towards the right-hand post, having left 'Tomorrow' well in the rear."

The old baronet exclaimed, "Rush the thing on! Flood the hoardings of London, Edinburgh, Manchester, Liverpool, Birmingham, Cardiff—all the large towns, and the smaller ones as well, if you can get hoardings big enough. Don't study the expense, either in the get-up or in the issue of the picture. Don't let the pill-sellers or cocoa or mustard people beat us."

The old man sprang to his feet and paced the floor, rubbing his hands, crying continually,

"Good! good! We'll wake old England up. We'll——"

"Toddle into lunch," interrupted George Carlyon. "That's the third summons we've had!"

Tom Hammond sat next to Madge at luncheon, and was charmed with her easy, unconventional manners. But his mind was too full of the new paper, of the great opportunity that had come to him so unexpectedly, to be as wholly absorbed with the charm of her personality as he might otherwise have been.

He did not linger over the luncheon table.

"There are one or two fellows, Sir Archibald," he explained, "whom I should like to secure on my staff at once. I don't want to lose even an hour."

As he bade Madge Finisterre good-bye, he expressed the hope that he might see her again soon, and the girl in reply allowed her eyes unconsciously to express more than her words.

"She is the most charming woman I ever met," he told himself, as he followed Sir Archibald into his room for the final word for which the baronet had asked. George Carlyon had remained behind with Madge.

"It was about the first working expenses I wanted to speak to you, Mr. Hammond," the baronet began. They were seated in the baronet's room.

"I will have fifty thousand pounds—or shall we say a

hundred thousand?—deposited, at once, in your name at
—what bank?"

"Any good bank you please, Sir Archibald, so long as
the particular branch is fairly central."

"Capital and Counties—how will that do?" the baronet
asked, adding, "I always bank with them myself."

"That will do, sir."

"How about the Ludgate Hill branch, Mr. Hammond?"

"Could not be better, sir."

"Settled, then, Mr. Hammond!" There were a few
more words exchanged between master and man, and
then they parted.

As Tom Hammond strode along the Embankment
towards Waterloo Bridge, his heart was the heart of a
boy again.

"Is life worth living!" he cried inwardly, answering
his own question with the rapturous words: "In this
hour I know nothing else that earth could give me to
make life more joyous!"

People passing him saw his face radiant with a wondrous joy. It's rare to see peace, even, in faces in our
great cities. It is rarer still to see joy's gleam. He
allowed his glance to flash all around him, as he murmured, "I am glad, too, that I am in London. Who
dare say that London is dull, or grim, or sordid? Who
was it that wrote, "No man curses the town more
heartily than I, but after travelling by mountains, plain,
desert, forest, and on the deep sea, one comes back to
London and finds it the most wonderful place of them
all!"

"Ah! It was Roger Pocock, I believe, wrote that
sentiment. Roger Pocock, 'I looks towards yer, sir.

Them's my senterments !' "

He laughed low and gleefully at his own merry mood. Then as his eyes took in the river, the moving panorama of the Embankment, and caught the throb of the mighty pulsing of life all about him, Le Gallienne's lines came to him, and, while he moved onward, he murmured:

> "London, whose loveliness is everywhere.
> London so beautiful at morning light,
> One half forgets how fair she is at night.
>
> "London as beautiful at set of sun
> As though her beauty had just begun!
> London, that mighty sob, that splendid tear,
> That jewel hanging in the great world's ear.
>
> "Ah! of your beauty change no single grace,
> My London with your sad mysterious face."

He moved forward in a strange rapture of spirit. He forgot even "beautiful London"; he was momentarily unconscious how he travelled or whither. He might have been blind or deaf for all that he now saw or heard. The drone of a blind beggar's voice reading the Scriptures, however, presently had power to break his trance. He paused a moment before the man.

"This same Jesus," droned the blind man's voice, "who is taken up from you into heaven, shall so come in like manner as ye have seen Him go."

Hammond dropped a sixpence into the beggar's box, and moved away, the wonder of the words he had just heard read arresting all his previous thoughts of his glad success.

"Shall so come in like manner!" he murmured. "I wonder what it means?"

The next instant a woman's pitiful voice filled his ear, crying:

"For the love of God, good sir, give me the price of a piece of bread."

He turned sharply towards her. Her face was haggard and hunger-filled; her eyes were wells of despair. He slipped his finger and thumb into the fob of his coat. The first coin that came to his touch was a shilling. He dropped it into the emaciated, outstretched palm.

The wretched creature gazed at the coin, then at him. Her lips moved, but no words came from them. Her eyes filled with a rush of tears. He passed on. But the incident moved him strangely.

"If Christ," he mused, "ever comes back to earth again, surely, surely He will deliver it from such want and misery as that!"

He paused and looked back at the woman. Her face was buried in her hands. Her form was shaking with sobs. Curiosity tempted him to go back.

As he came abreast of her, a child, a girl about nine, barefooted and tired-looking, was saying to the woman, "What's the matter, missis? Wouldn't that swell giv' yer nuffink w'en yer arst 'im?"

"Give me nothing?" The woman glanced down at the child. "Why, he is kinder than Gawd, fur he give me a shilling!"

At this Tom Hammond hurried away.

"Kinder than God!" he murmured. "Oh, God, that we should have it in our power to buy such happiness for so small a sum!"

"Kinder than God" he repeated to himself. He was now mounting the granite steps to the bridge. "Of course, one knows better; yet how difficult of proof it would become, if one had to explain it to that poor soul, and to the thousands like her in this great city!"

For the first time since leaving Sir Archibald his own joy was forgotten. The awful problem of London's destitution had supplanted London's beauty in his thoughts.

CHAPTER III.

FLOTSAM.

"ONLY nine hours!"

Tom Hammond laughed amusedly at his own murmured thought. It seemed ridiculous almost to try to believe that only nine hours before he had been a discharged journalist, while now he was at the head of what he knew would be the greatest journalistic venture London—yea, the world—had ever seen.

He had just dined. He felt that he wanted some kind of movement, some distraction, to relieve the tension. He was in that frame of mind when some kind of adventure was necessary, although he did not tell himself this, being hardly conscious of his own need. He knew that the haunts of his fellows—club, theatre, music-hall—would only serve to irritate him. Some instinct turned his feet riverwards.

It was now a quarter past seven o'clock. Night had fallen upon London. Tom Hammond crossed the great Holborn thoroughfare. The heavier traffic of London's commercial life had almost ceased. The omnibuses going west were filled with theatregoers, and other pleasure-seekers. Hansoms flitted swiftly either way, each holding a man and a woman in evening dress.

Having crossed the roadway, he paused for a moment at the corner of Chancery Lane, and let his eye take in all the scene. And again Le Gallienne came to his mind, and he softly murmured:

"Ah! London! London! our delight,
Great flower that opens but at night,
Great city of the midnight sun,
Whose day begins when day is done.

"Lamp after lamp against the sky
Opens a sudden beaming eye,
Leaping alight on every hand,
The iron lilies of the Strand,

"Like dragonflies the hansoms hover
With jewelled eyes to catch the lover;
The streets are full of lights and loves,
Soft gowns and flutter of soiled doves."

He turned with a faint sigh, and began to pass on down Chancery Lane.

"Oh, London!" he mused, "thy surface may be wonderful and beautiful; but below—what are you below the surface?"

"The human moths about the light
Dash and cling in dazed delight,
And burn and laugh, the world and wife,
For this is London, this is life!

"Upon thy petals butterflies,
But at thy root, some say, there lies
A world of weeping, trodden things,
Poor worms that have not eyes or wings."

He moved onwards in the direction of the Law Courts. Presently he neared the Waterloo Bridge approach. He had, all unrealized by himself, since he left the restaurant where he had dined, been walking towards the river. A moment or two after, and he was leaning on the parapet of the bridge, looking down into the dark waters. Sluggish, oil-like in appearance, as seen in the dull gleam of the lamps, the river moved seawards. A sudden longing to get out upon those dark waters came to him.

"If only——" he mused. Then, turning briskly, he came face to face with a man in a blue guernsey, who was crossing the bridge. It was the very man of his half-uttered thought. "If only I could run up against Bob Carter!" he had almost said.

"Good evening, Mister Ham'nd." The man in the guernsey saluted with a thick, tar-stained forefinger as he recognized Tom Hammond.

"Good evening, Carter." Hammond laughed as he added, "I was just wishing I could meet you, for I felt I should like to get out on the river."

"I'm jes' going as fur as Lambeff, sir. Ef yer likes ter go wif me, you'll do me proud, sir; yer know that, I knows!"

A few minutes later the two men sat in Carter's boat. Hammond, in the stern, was steering. The man Carter, on the first thwart, manipulated the oars. Hammond had known the man about a year. He had done him a kindness that the waterman had never forgotten.

"Aw'd go to ther world's end fur yer, sir," he had often said since.

The man was ordinarily a silent companion, and tonight after a few exchanged words between the pair, he was as silent as usual.

Down the wide, turgid river the boat, propelled by Carter's two oars, shot jerkily, the rise and fall of the glow in the rower's pipe-bowl synchronizing with the lift and dip of the oars.

Hammond enjoyed the silence. There was a weirdness about this night trip on the river that fitted in with his mood. His brain had been considerably overwrought that day. The quiet row was beginning to soothe the overwrought nerves. Where he sat in the

stern of the boat, he faced the clock-tower at Westminster. The gleaming windows of the great embankment hotels lay behind him. A myriad electric lights
were on his right hand. The gloom and darkness of the
unlighted wharfage on the Surrey side were on his left.

Only by a waterway miracle Carter cleared an anchored
barge that, defying the laws of the river, carried no
warning light.

"Drat 'em!" growled the man Carter. "They oughter
do a stretch in Portlan' or Dartmoor fur breakin' the
lor. There's many a 'onest waterman whose boat's foun'
bottom-up, or smashed to smithereens, an' whose body's
foun', or isn't, jes, as the case may be, all becos' they
lazy houn's is too 'ide-boun' to light a lamp, cuss 'em!"

His growl died away in his throat. The glowing fire
of his pipe rose and fell quicker than ever, telling of a
fierce anger burning within him.

Ssh!" he hissed. Hammond saw that his face was
turned shorewards. He heaved aft towards Hammond,
and whispered, "Kin yer see that woman, sir?" He
jerked his chin in the direction of a line of moored
barges.

Hammond had turned his head, and could plainly
discern the form of a woman standing on the edge of
the outer barge of the cluster.

The men in the boat sat still, but watchful.

"Do she mean sooerside, sir?" whispered Carter.
"Looks like it, sir. Don't make a soun'."

Even as he spoke the woman leaped into the air.
There was a low scream, a splash, a leap of foam flashed
dully for one instant, then all was still again.

The waterman plied his oars furiously. Hammond
steered for the spot where that foam had splashed. An

instant later the boat was over the place where the body had disappeared. Carter lay on his oars, and peered into the darkness on one side. Hammond strained his eye on the other side.

With startling suddenness a hand darted upwards within a foot of where Hammond sat in the stern of the boat. In the same instant the woman's head appeared. Hammond reached out excitedly, and caught the back hair of the woman, twisting his fingers securely into the knot of hair at the back of her head.

Carter shipped his oars, and in two minutes the wretched woman was safe in the boat. Her drenched face gleamed white where they laid her. A low whimpering sob broke from her.

"Turn 'er over on her face a little, sir, while I makes the boat fast fur a minute or two, sir," jerked out the waterman.

"Pore soul ov 'er!" he went on, knotting his painter to a bolt in the stern of a barge. "She 'ave took in a bellyful of Thames water, an' it ain't filtered no sort, that's sartin!"

Hammond had by this time turned the woman over on her face.

Carter came aft bearing a water-beaker in his hands.

"I'll lift her legs, sir," he said, and you put this beaker under her, jes' above her knees; that'll 'elp her a bit."

That was done, and almost instantly the woman was very sick.

"In my locker there, sir, I've got a drop o' whisky. I keeps it there fur 'mergencies like this," said Carter.

Hammond moved to allow the man to reach a seat-locker in the stern. The next minute, while Hammond supported the woman, the waterman poured a few drops of the spirit down her throat.

She coughed and sputtered, but the draught restored her. She began to cry in a low, whimpering way.

"We must get her ashore, Carter," cried Hammond. "I'll take the oars, and, as you know the riverside better than I do, just steer into the nearest landing-place you know."

Carter leaped to the bows, cast off the painter, and hurried aft again.

"Jes' 'long yere, sir, there's an old landin' as'll jes' serve us. Wots yer fink ter do wi' the pore soul, sir—not 'and her over to the perlice?"

"No, neither the police nor workhouse, Carter. I wish I could see her face, and see what kind of woman she is."

By way of reply, Carter struck a match, and lit a small bull's-eye lantern. When the wick had caught light, he flashed it on the face of the woman.

Her eyes were closed, her face was deadly pale. Her hair was dishevelled. But in the one flashing glance Hammond took at her, he recognized her.

"It's Mrs. Joyce!" he muttered half-aloud and in amazed tones.

"Know 'er, sir?" asked the waterman.

"A little!" he replied "Her husband is a reporter—a drinking scamp."

Carter shut off the light of the bull's-eye, at that moment.

"We're jes' 'ere now, sur, so's best not to be callin' 'tention like wi' a light."

He steered the boat into a kind of narrow alley-way between two crazy old wharves

*   *   *   *   *   *   *

Hammond, rightly gauging the kindly heart of his landlady, had brought the drenched woman in a cab to his lodgings. She was still in a half-fainting condition when he carried her into the house. In two sentences he explained the situation to the landlady, whose natural kindness and loyalty to her lodger made her willing to aid his purpose of rescue.

"I will carry her up to the bath-room," he said. "Let your girl get a cup of milk heated as hot as can be sipped, while you bath this poor soul quickly in very hot water. Then let her be got to bed, and have some good, nourishing soup ready. She'll probably sleep after that. And in the morning—well, the events of the morning will take their own shape."

Half-an-hour later, as Hammond took a cup of coffee, he had the satisfaction of knowing that the woman he had saved was in bed, and doing well.

"Poor soul!" he mused. "That brute of a husband has probably driven her to this attempt on her life. I wonder what her history was before she married, for I remember how it struck me, that day when I saw her at the office, that she was evidently a woman of some culture."

It was nearly ten now. He had no desire to go out again. It wanted two hours quite to his usual bed-time. But a strange sense of drowsiness began to steal over him, and he went off to his bed.

"What a day this has been!" he muttered, as he laid his head on the pillow.

CHAPTER IV.

"I ONLY REAPED WHAT I SOWED."

HAMMOND awaited the woman whom he had saved from drowning.

"She has slept fairly well," the landlady told him, "and I made her eat a good breakfast that I carried up to her myself, Mr. Hammond!"

Now he waited to speak to her. A moment or two more, and the landlady ushered her into the room, then slipped away.

"How can I ever repay you, sir!" cried the woman, seizing the hand that Hammond held out to her.

For a moment or two her emotion was too great for further speech. Hammond led her to an armchair and seated her. She sobbed convulsively for a moment or two. He allowed her to sob. Presently tears came. The paroxysm passed, the tears relieved her, and she lifted her sad, beautiful eyes to his face.

"You know—oh, yes, you must know, Mr. Hammond —(I recognized you last night)—how I came to be in the water. I tried to take my life. I was miserable, despairing! God forgive me."

His strong eyes were full of a rare tenderness, as he said, "But, Mrs. Joyce, you surely know that death is not the end of all existence. I am not what would be called a religious man, but every fibre of my inward being tells me that death does not end all."

He saw a shiver pass over her, as she hoarsely replied, "I, too, realize that this morning, Mr. Hammond. But last night the madness of an overwhelming despair was upon me. My life had been a literal hell for years, until yesterday I could bear it no longer. I was famished with hunger, sick with despair, and——"

She sighed wearily. "Perhaps," she went on, "if you knew all I have borne, you would not wonder at my rash, mad act."

"Tell me your story, Mrs. Joyce," he said, gently. "It may relieve your overcharged heart, and, anyhow, I will be your friend, as far as I can."

She sighed again. This time there was a note of relief, rather than weariness, in the sigh.

"My father was a well-to-do farmer," she began, "in North Hants. I was the only child, and I fear I was spoiled. I received the best education possible, and loved my studies for their own sake, for culture, in all its forms, had a strong attraction for me. I had been engaged to a young yeoman farmer for nearly a year. I had known him all my life, and we had been sweethearts even as children. Then there came suddenly into my life that man Joyce, for whom I sacrificed everything. God only knows how he contrived to exercise such an awful fascination over me as to make me leave everyone, everything, and marry him."

For a moment she paused, and shuddered. Her voice, when she spoke, again, was hollow, and full of tears.

"I killed my father by eloping on the very eve of my arranged marriage with Ronald Ferris. Ronald left the country as soon as he could wind up his affairs. And I—well, here in this mighty Babylon, I have ever since been reaping some of the sorrow I had sown. Not a penny of my father's money ever reached me, and that brute Joyce only married me for what he expected to get with me. He has done his best to make earth a hell for me, and I, in my mad blindness, last night, almost exchanged earth's fleeting hell for God's eternal hell."

A look of shame filled her eyes as she lifted them to Hammond.

"What you reminded me of just now, Mr. Hammond, I, deep down in my soul, know only too well —that death does not end all. My father was a true Christian, and a lay preacher. I have travelled with him hundreds of times to his preaching appointments, playing the harmonium and singing solos for him in his services. More than once the sense of God's claim upon me was so great as almost to compel my yielding my heart and life. Would to God I had! But my pride, my ambitions, strangled my good desires, and, as I said just now, I broke my father's heart. I killed him, and ruined all my own life, though I have no pity for myself. Then London life, my husband's brutality, my own misery, all helped to drive even the memory of God from my mind."

"Yet," broke in Hammond, "the Christian religion teaches that sorrow and suffering ought to drive the possessor of the faith nearer to God."

There was a hint of apology in his tones as he went on :

"Don't misunderstand me, Mrs. Joyce; I only speak from hearsay. I have heard parsons preach it, but I know nothing experimentally about these things myself."

She smiled in a slow, sad way, and, catching her breath in a kind of quick sob, said : "Neither have I ever known anything experimentally of these truths. I drifted into the outward form of a correct, religious,

life. I learned to like the brightness of our chapel
services, the fun of choir practice, the merry company,
the adulation heaped upon me for my solo-singing. Then
there were the tea-meetings, the service of song, and
a multitude of other mild excitements which went to
brighten the monotony of a rural existence. But of
God, of Christ, of the Divine life, I fear I knew
nothing."

Hammond smiled inwardly as he listened to this strange
confession. The phraseology was new to him.

"It is the shibboleth of Nonconformity, I suppose," he
told himself. "And I suppose each section of religious
society has its own outward form of things in which
it trusts, thinking, caring, nothing for the great Divine
verities that should be the true religious life."

He did not utter his thoughts aloud, but asked with
some apparent irrelevance, "Where is your husband,
Mrs. Joyce?"

"Off on one of his drinking bouts, or maybe, locked
up for drunkenness; I cannot say."

Her lifted eyes were full of beseeching, as she went
on, "You will keep secret, Mr. Hammond, all this wild,
mad episode of my life. If only I could know that the
sad, mad, bad story was locked up between God and
you, your kind landlady and myself, I think I could go
back and face my misery better."

"Do not fear, Mrs. Joyce," he replied quickly. "The
affair shall be as though it had never been. I can answer
for Mrs. Belcher, my landlady; and for myself I give
you my word, and——"

"God reward you, sir!" she sobbed. "Already you
have given me clearer views of Him than any minister
or any sermon ever did."

A few moments later Mrs. Joyce rose to leave. He pressed three sovereigns into her hand, and in spite of her tearful protestations made her take the money.

"If you are ever in desperate need, come to me, or write me, Mrs. Joyce, and I will help you, if I can. Meanwhile, be assured that the little I have done for you I would have done for any stranger, for, after all, the human race is linked by a strange, a mighty family tie. Good-bye."

She wrung the hand he gave her, then with a sudden, impulsive movement she lifted it sharply to her lips and kissed it with a tearful passionateness.

The next moment she was gone. His hand was wet with her tears.

"Poor soul!" he muttered.

Passing across the room to the window, he glanced out. She was moving down the street. Her handkerchief was pressed to her eyes.

"How strange," he murmured, as he turned from the window, "are these chance encounters in life! Like ships at sea, we sight, hail, exchange some kind of greeting, then pass on. Do we, after all, I wonder, unconsciously influence each other in these apparently trivial life-encounters? If so, how? Take this episode now, for instance. Will my encounter with that poor soul have any effect on my life, or on hers? If so, what?

CHAPTER V.

LILY WORK.

THE room we now enter is a large one. It is clos[e] under the roof of a house in Finsbury. The ma[n] there at work pauses for a moment.

The room is a workshop. The man is a Jew—bu[t] what a Jew! He might have posed to an artist as [a] model, a type of the proudest Jewish monarch ove[r] Israel. Face, form, stature—not even Saul or David [or] Solomon could have excelled him.

The room held the finished workmanship of his han[d] for the three past years. And now, as he paused i[n] his labour—a labour of love—for a moment, and dre[w] his tall form erect, and lifted his face to the windo[w] above him, a lignt that was almost holy filled his eyes.

"God of our fathers," he murmured, "God of t[he] Holy Tent and of the Temple, instruct me; teach m[y] fingers to do this great work."

He let his hands fall with an almost sacred touc[h] upon the chapter he had been chasing. He wist n[ot] that his face shone with an unearthly light, as for [a] moment his lips moved in prayer. Then quietly reac[h]ing a thick old book from a shelf, he opened it at on[e] of its earlier pages, and read aloud.

"And the Lord spake unto Moses, saying, See, [I] have called by name Bezaleel, the son of Uri, the s[on] of Hur, of the tribe of Judah: and I have filled hi[m] with the Spirit of God, in wisdom, and in understan[d]ing, and in knowledge, and in all manner of workma[n]ship, to devise cunning works, to work in gold, and silver, and in brass, and in cutting of stones, to set them, and in carving of timber, to work in all kinds of workmanship. And I, behold, I have given with him Aholiab, the son of Ahisamach, of the tribe of Dan: and in the hearts of all that are wise-hearted I have put wisdom, that they may make all that I have commanded thee: the tabernacle of the congregation, and the ark of the testimony, and the mercy-seat that is thereupon, and all the furniture of the tabernacle."

The light—it was now almost a fire—deepened in his eyes. A rare, a rich, cadence filled his voice as he read the holy words. His fingers moved to the middle of the book. It easily opened at a certain place, as though it had been often used at that page. Again he read aloud:

"And the chapiters that were upon the top of the pillars were of lily work,............and the chapiters upon the two pillars had pomegranates also above,............and the pomegranates were two hundred, in rows round about upon the other chapiter,............and he set up the pillars in the porch of the temple: and he set up the right pillar, and called the name thereof Jachin ("He shall establish"); and he set up the left pillar, and called the name thereof Boaz ("In it is strength"). And on the top of the pillars was lily work: so was the work of the pillars finished."

With a reverent touch the man closed the book, replaced it on the shelf, then, lifting his eyes again to where the cold, clear light streamed down through the great skylight in the ceiling, he murmured:

"How long, O Lord, shall Thy people be cast off and trodden down, and their land, Thy land, be held by the accursed races?"

For a moment a look of pain swept into his face. Then, as he became conscious of the touch of his lowered hand upon the chapiter, his eyes travelled downwards to the exquisite "lily work," and the light of a new hope swept the pain off his face.

"The very fact that the time has come," he murmured, "for us to be preparing for the next temple, is a token from Jehovah that the day of Messiah draweth nigh."

His eyes lingered a moment on the rare and beautiful workmanship, then he took up a chasing tool and continued his toil; yet, while he worked he kept up a running recitative of Ezekiel's description of the great temple—for he knew by heart all the chapters of that prophet.

As he presently repeated the words: "And the Prince in the midst of them, when they go in, shall go in; and when they go forth, shall go forth," he lifted his eyes with a deep holy rapture shining in all his face.

He closed his recitative with a ringing note of triumph in his voice, as he cried, "It shall be round about eighteen thousand cubits: and the name of the city from that day shall be Jehovah-Chammah"—"The Lord is there."

There was a moment of absolute silence. The graver was still, the hand that held it might have been stone, so rigid did it become. The lips of Abraham Cohen moved, but no other sound came from him save the words "Jehovah was there," and he prayed aloud.

In the midst of his rapt devotion the door of the workroom opened. The slight sound aroused the dreamer. He turned his face in the direction of the door, and his eyes flashed with pleasure.

"Ah, Zillah!" he cried in greeting. The girl he addressed closed the door, thus shutting out the odour of frying fish. She crossed the floor quickly, with a certain eagerness, and came towards him with a rare grace. She was singularly beautiful, of an Eastern style of beauty. Her complexion was of the Spanish olive tone, and her melting eyes were of that same Spanish type. Her hair—a wondrous crown of it—was blue-black. She had a certain plumpness of form that seemed to add rather than take from her general beauty. She was sister to his wife.

"Supper will be ready in five minutes, Abraham," she began. "Will you be ready for it?"

He smiled down into her great black eyes. He was never very keen on his meals. He ate to live only; he did not live to eat. She knew that, and had long since learned that his labour of love was as meat and drink to him. Her eyes glided past him and rested on his work.

"It is very beautiful, Abraham!" she cried. There was reverence as well as rapture and admiration in her voice and glance.

"It cannot be too beautiful, Zillah," he returned.

Her eyes were on his work. His were on her face. He read in it the rapturous admiration of his workmanship.

"When will the Messiah come?" she sighed.

"Soon, I believe!" he returned. "Jehovah rested in His creative work after six days' labour. A thousand years with Him are as one day. May it not well be, then, that as there have passed nearly six thousand years (each thousand years, representing one day) that He will presently rest in His finished work for His people, through the coming of the Messiah, as He did at the creation?"

He laid his tool aside, and turned to the beautiful girl, as he continued:

"Besides, do not our sacred books say that when three springs have been discovered on Mount Zion, Messiah will come? Two springs have lately been discovered by the excavators in Jerusalem, and our people out there excitedly watch the work of these men, expecting soon the discovery of the third spring."

Her eager, parted lips told how she hung upon his speech. He smiled down gratefully into her great black lustrous eyes, though a sigh escaped him as he said:

"Ah! I wish Leah would only show a little of the interest in all this, that you do, Zillah!"

"You must not blame Leah too much, Abraham," the girl answered quickly. "She has her children, you know. Mother always said that if ever Leah had babies, that there would be nothing else in the world for her except the babies. Besides, Abraham, no two of us are constituted alike, and Leah is what the Gentiles about here call happy-go-lucky. But, Abraham, tell me more of what you think of Messiah's coming. Leah's five minutes will be sure to run to a quarter of an hour."

"I do think Messiah is coming soon," cried the young fellow excitedly. "Who knows? Perhaps when the Passover comes again, and we set His chair, and open the door for Him to enter, that He will suddenly come. Did I tell you, Zillah, about the date discovery at Safed, in Palestine?"

"No, what is it?" The girl's face glowed with a strange earnestness, her voice rang with it.

"Safed," he went on, quickly, "is a little town to the north-west of Galilee. Our Rabbi there has discovered from our sacred books, that Messiah's coming, and the overthrow of our enemies, will be in the year five thousand six hundred and sixty-six—nineteen hundred and six according to the Gentile reckoning. Our Father Moses, and all the children of Israel sang, when Jehovah delivered them from the Red Sea:—'Yea, by the force of Thy swelling waves hast Thou demolished those who arose against Thee. Thou didst discharge Thy wrath, it devoured them up like stubble.' Our Rabbis—and even the Christian Gentile teachers—agree that the deliverance of our race from Pharaoh, and the destruction of his hosts, picture our race's future as well as its past. And the numerical value of 'Thou shalt overthrow' (part of those two song-stanzas I have just repeated) gives the date I have mentioned as the time of our deliverance from all our troubles, when Messiah shall come."

There was a sudden clatter of little feet outside at that moment, and a boy and a girl burst into the room.

"What do you think, father?" cried the boy, with the excited impulsiveness of a child bursting with news. "A boy—he's a Gentile, of course—whom I know says that Messiah has come, that the cursed Nazarene was He, and that——"

"We will go to supper, Reuben, and you and I will talk about that another time." Cohen spoke quietly to his boy. He had his own reasons for checking the subject at that time.

His aunt caught the boy's hand, and danced with him out of the room. Rachel, the little girl, a wondrous miniature of Zillah, clung to her father, and the whole family trooped off to wash their hands before the meal.

CHAPTER VI.

AN INTERESTING TALK.

"THE Courier" was now an established fact. As a newspaper it was as much a revelation to the journalists as to the general public. London had taken to it from the first moment of its issue. The provinces, instead of following their usual course of waiting to see what London did, took their own initiative, and adopted the new paper at once. Every instinct about the ideal paper, felt and nursed during the waiting years by Tom Hammond, had been true instinct. He had always felt them to be true; now he realized the fact. He was a proud man, a happy man.

One curious feature of the new journal had attracted much attention, even before the publication of the first issue. In his "Foreword," as he had termed it, in a full page announcement that appeared in three of the leading London dailies, Tom Hammond had said:

"An important feature of the 'Courier' will be the item or items (as the case may be) which will be found each day under the heading, 'From the Prophet's Chamber.' A greater man than the editor of 'The Courier' once said, 'Every editor of a newspaper ought to have a strain of the seer in his composition. He ought to have the gift of prophecy up to a certain point. He ought to be so thoroughly conversant with the history of his own and every other nation that when history is on the point of repeating itself—as it has a habit of doing,—he may not be caught altogether napping.' It is the unexpected that happens, we say.

True, but there are many of the so-called happenings of the unexpected that to the spirit of the seer will have been expected and more than half-prophesied.

Now, while we propose that the whole tone of 'The Courier' shall show the spirit of the seer in a measure, we shall endeavour to make the particular column to which we are now alluding essentially new. In it we shall deal with every class of subject likely to prove mentally arrestive to our readers, and shall make it prophetic up to the limits of our capacities as man, citizen and editor. How far the possession of the quality of the seer will be found in us we must leave the future—and our readers—to decide. But we certainly anticipate that 'The Prophet's Chamber' column will be one of the most popular features of what we shall aim to make the most popular paper of the day."

Tom Hammond was no believer in luck. He had left nothing to chance in the production of his paper. There was not a department left to subordinates which he did not personally assure himself was being carried out on the best, the safest, lines. For weeks he literally lived on the spot where his great paper was to be produced, taking his meals and sleeping at an hotel close by the huge building that housed "The Courier."

He saw very little of Sir Archibald Carlyon during these weeks, and nothing at all of George, or the fair American, Madge Finisterre. George was in Scotland; Madge on the Continent.

His thoughts often turned to the American girl, and

his eye brightened and his pulse quickened whenever he heard of her from Sir Archibald.

Once he had been permitted by Sir Archibald to read a gossipy letter sent by her to the old baronet. He laughed over a quotation in that letter.

"I am not like the Chicago girl," she wrote, "of whom our Will Carleton writes, who, telling all about her tour in 'Urop,' says,

> "Old Scotland? Yes, all in our power,
> We did there to be through;
> We stopped in Glasgow one whole hour,
> Then straight to 'Edinborough.'
> At Abbotsford we made a stay
> Of half-an-hour precisely.
> (The ruins all along the way
> Were ruined very nicely.)
>
> "We 'did' a mountain in the rain,
> And left the others undone,
> Then took the 'Flying Scotchman' train,
> And came by night to London.
> Long tunnels somewhere on the line
> Made sound and darkness deeper;
> No; English scenery is not fine
> Viewed from a Pullman sleeper.
>
> "Oh, Paris! Paris! Paris! 'Tis
> No wonder, dear, that you go
> So far into ecstasies
> About that Victor Hugo!
> He paints the city, high and low,
> With faithful pen and ready.
> (I think, my dear, I ought to know,
> We drove there two hours steady.")

"I feel," Madge had written, "that one wants a lifetime to 'do' the Continent."

Tom Hammond's thoughts often flew to the gay girl. This morning, having seen a review of Carleton's latest book of ballads, he had been reminded of her, and he laid down his pen a moment, as he gave himself up to a little reverie about her. An announcement aroused him.

"Miss Finisterre and Mr. Carlyon, sir."

He smiled to himself. "Talk of angels, etc.," he mused.

The next moment he was greeting his callers. Madge Finisterre looked, in Tom Hammond's eyes, more radiant now than ever.

"Fancy, Mr. Hammond," she laughed, when the greetings were over, "George and I met at Dover! He had come south to see a friend off from Dover, and was on the pier when I landed from the Calais boat. We've been down to that dear old country house, but I wanted to do some shopping, and to see how you looked as editor-in-chief and general boss of the biggest daily paper in the world."

Tom Hammond's eyes flashed with a pleased light at her confession, which implied that she had thought of him, even as he had thought of her. He noted, too, how an extra shade of colour warmed the clear skin of her cheeks as she made her confession.

"Because," she went on, "all the world declares that 'The Courier' is the premier paper of the world, and everyone who is anyone—in the know of things, I mean —knows that Mr. Tom Hammond is 'The Courier.'"

The talk, for a few minutes, was "shop."

"You don't go in for a column of comic," Madge presently said. "If you did, I could give you an item, we, George and I, heard in the train as we ran up to town. There were two of your English parsons in our carriage, talking in that high-faluting note that always reminds me of your high-pitched church service,—'dearly-beloved-brethren' note.

"Well, the two parsons were telling yarns one against

the other—chestnuts were cheap, I assure you,—and one of them told a story he tacked on to General Booth— the last time I heard it, it was told of Spurgeon. He said that the General was going down Whitechapel, and, seeing the people pouring into a show, and wondering what there was so powerfully attractive to the masses in these shows, he determined to go into this particular one. It was advertised as a 'Museum of Biblical Curiosities.' Just as he got in, the showman was exhibiting a very rusty old sword, and saying,

"'Now, yere's a werry hinterestin' hobject. This is the sword wot Balaam 'it 'is hass wiv, 'cos 'ee wouldn't go.' Booth speaks up, and says,

"'Hold hard there, my friend; you're getting a little mixed. Balaam hadn't got a sword. He said, "Would that I had a sword."'

"'That's all right, guv'nor,' cried the showman; 'this is the sword 'ee wished 'ee 'ad.'"

The girl's mimicry of the coster-showman's speech was inimitable, and the two men laughed as much at her telling as at the tale itself.

George Carlyon got up from his seat, saying, "But I say, you two, do you mind if I leave you to amuse each other for an hour? I want, very much, to run down to the club. I'll come back for you, Madge, or meet you somewhere."

"Bless the boy!" she laughed. "Do you think I was reared in an incubator, or in your Mayfair? Haven't you learned that, given a Yankee girl's got dollars under her boots to wheel on, it ain't much fuss for her to skate through this old country of yours, nor yet through Europe, come to that, even though she has no more languages under her tongue than good plain Duchess county American. I told the 'boys' that before I left home."

George Carlyon laughed, as, accepting his release, he nodded to the pair and left the room.

It was a strangely new experience to Tom Hammond, to be left alone with a beautiful and charming woman like Madge Finisterre.

The picture she made, as she moved round the room looking at the framed paintings, all gifts from his artist friends, came to him as a kind of revelation. When he had met her that day in the Embankment hotel, he had been charmed with her beauty and her frank, open, unconventionality of manner. He had thought of her many times since—only that very day, a moment before her arrival,—thought of her as men think of a picture or a poem which has given them delight. But now he found her appealing to him.

She was a woman, a beautiful, attractive woman. She suggested sudden thoughts of how a woman, loved, and returning that love, might affect his life, his happiness.

Her physical grace and beauty, the exquisite fit of her costume, the perfect harmony of it—all this struck him now. But the woman in her appealed strongest to him.

"Awfully good, this sketch of street arabs!" she turned to say, as she stood before a clever bit of black-and-white drawing.

An end of a lace scarf she was wearing caught in a nail in the wall. He sprang forward to release the scarf. It was not readily done, for his fingers became infected with a strange nervousness. Once their hands met, their fingers almost interlocked. A curious little thrill went through him. He lifted his eyes involuntarily, and met her glance. A warm colour shot swiftly into her face. And he was conscious at the same moment that his own cheeks burned.

"I guess I'll sit down before I do any more mischief," she laughed.

Woman-like, she was quicker to get at ease than he was.

"Do you know, Mr. Hammond," she went on, as she seated herself in a revolving armchair, "I just wanted very much to see how you were fixed up here, and how you looked now that you are a big man."

He made a deprecatory little gesture.

"Oh, but you are a really great man," she went on. "I have heard some big people talk of you, and say ——"

She leaned back, and smiled merrily at him, as she went on,

"Well, I guess if there's only a shadow of truth in the old saying, then your ears must often have burned."

Madge Finisterre gave the chair in which she was sitting a half twist.

"Why don't you British people go in for rockers?" she asked. "I simply can't enjoy your English homes to the full, for want of a good rocker, wherever I go."

An indiarubber bulb lay close to his hand. He pressed it without her noting the movement. A clerk suddenly appeared. Hammond looked across at Madge, with an "Excuse me, Miss Finisterre, one moment."

He drew a sheet of notepaper towards him. The paper was headed with "The Courier" title and address.

"Send me, at once, unpacked and ready for immediate use, the best American drawing-room rocking-chair you have in stock. Send invoice, cash will follow," etc.

That was what he wrote. He enclosed it in an envelope, then on a separate slip of paper he wrote:—

"Take a cab, there and back, to Wallis's, Holborn Circus. See how smart you can be; bring the chair, ordered, back with you."

From his purse he took a four-shilling piece, and gave the young fellow the note, the slip of instructions, and the coin.

As the attendant left the room, he turned again to Madge, who, utterly unsuspicious of the errand on which he had sent his employee, was amusing herself with a copy of "Punch." She looked up from the paper as the door closed.

"I like 'The Courier' immensely, Mr. Hammond," she cried. There was a rare warmth of admiration in her tone.

"Thank you, Miss Finisterre!" His eyes said more than his words, "what do you specially like in it ?" he asked; "or is your liking of a more general character?"

"I do like it from a general standpoint," she replied; "I think it the best paper in the world. But especially do I like your own particular column, 'From a Prophet's Chamber.' But, Mr. Hammond, about the Jew—you are going in strong for him, aren't you?"

"From the ordinary newspaper point, yes," he said. "I cannot quite recall how my mind was first switched on to the subject, but I do know this—that the more I study the past history of the race, and the future predictions concerning it, the more amazed I am, how, past, present, and future, the Jews, as a nation, are interwoven with everything political, musical, artistic—everything, in fact. And I wonder, equally, that we journalists, as a whole—I speak, of course, as far as I know my kinsmen in letters—should have thought and written so little about them.

"Take their ubiquitousness, Miss Finisterre," went on Hammond. "There does not appear to have been an empire in the past that has not had its colony of Jews. By which I do not mean a Ghetto, simply, a herding of sordid-living, illiterate Hebrews, but a study colony of men and women, who, by sheer force of intellect, of brain power, have obtained and maintained the highest positions, the greatest influence.

"Why, in China, even, isolated, conservative China, before Christ was born in Bethlehem, the Jews were a prosperous, ubiquitous people, worshipping the one God, Jehovah, amidst all the foulness of Chinese idolatries."

Madge Finisterre listened with rapt interest. The man before her, fired with his subject, talked marvellously. A good listener helps to make a good talker, and Tom Hammond talked well.

"It is not simply that they practically hold the wealth of the world in their hands, that they are the world's bankers, but they are dominating our press, our politics."

With glowing picture of words he poured out a flood of wondrous fact and illustration, winding up presently with:

"Then you cannot kill the Jew, you cannot wipe him out. Persecution has had the effect of stunting his growth, so that the average Britisher is several inches taller than the average Jew. But the life of the Hebrew is indestructible. Sometimes of late I have asked myself this question, as I have reviewed the history of the dealings of so-called Christianity with the Semitic race—Has Christianity been afraid of the Jews, or why has she sought to stamp them out?"

The pair had been so engrossed with their talk that they had lost all count of time. A half-hour had slipped by since Tom Hammond had sent his messenger to Wallis's. The young fellow suddenly appeared at the door.

"Got it, Charlie?"

Without waiting for a reply to his question, the editor bounded from his seat and passed outside. Thirty seconds later the door opened again, and he appeared, bearing a splendid rocker in his arms.

Before she fully realized the wonder of the whole thing, Madge found herself seated in the rocking-chair. Swaying backwards and forwards, and blushing and smiling, she cried:

"You are a wonderful man, Mr. Hammond!"

"You said you could never fully enjoy our English houses for want of a rocker. Now, however 'angelic' your visits to this room may be, you shall have one inducement to slip in—a rocker."

She was beginning her thanks again, when he interrupted with:

"But, excuse me, Miss Finisterre, what about some tea? Shall we go out and get some, or would you prefer that I should order it in here?"

"Oh, here, by all means! I can have tea at a restaurant every day of my life, but with a real London lion—a real live editor—and in his own special den. Why, it may never fall to my lot again. Oh, here, by all means!" she cried, excitedly.

He squeezed that rubber bulb again. To the lad Charlie, who appeared, he gave a written order to a neighbouring restaurant. Twenty minutes later the tea was in the room.

Madge officiated with the teapot. Hammond watched her every movement. A truly pretty, graceful girl never looks handsomer to a man than when presiding at a tea-table. Tom Hammond thought Madge had never looked more charming. The meal was a very enjoyable one, and as she poured out his second cup he paid her a pretty compliment, adding:

"To see you thus, Miss Finisterre, makes one think what fools men are not to——"

He paused abruptly. She flashed a quick glance of enquiry at him.

"Not to what, Mr. Hammond?"

"I wonder," he replied, "if I ought to say what I left unsaid?"

"Why not?" she asked.

"I don't know why I should not," he laughed. "I was going to say that, to have a bright, beautiful, grace-ful woman like Madge Finisterre pouring out tea for him, makes a man think what a fool he is not to marry."

His tone and glance were alike full of meaning. She could not mistake him. Her colour heightened visibly. Her eyes drooped before his ardent gaze. The situation became tense and full of portent.

The opening of the door at that instant changed every-thing. George Carlyon had returned. At the same moment a wire was brought to Hammond, together with a sheaf of letters—the afternoon mail.

CHAPTER VII.

"COMING."

GEORGE Carlyon's entrance, the arrival of the afternoon mail, and the telegram gave Madge Finisterre an opportunity to escape. George Carlyon was anxious to leave, and Madge rose at once to accompany him.

Tom Hammond did not press them to stay, for he, too, felt awkward. The friends shook hands. The eyes of Madge and Hammond met for one instant. Each face flushed under the power of the other's glance.

When the door had closed upon them, Tom went back to his old place by the table, his eyes involuntarily sweeping the whole apartment. He smiled as he suddenly realized how empty the room now seemed. His glance rested upon the tea-tray, and he rang for the lad Charlie.

"Clear all this away, Charlie, please," he began. Then with a smile he said, "You will find a capital cup of tea in that pot."

The boy grinned. At his first glance at the tray he had mentally decided that he would be able to have a rare feast. A couple of minutes, and the boy had gone.

Tom Hammond gathered up his mail, and was about to drop into his ordinary seat, when he remembered the rocker. With a smile at Madge's occupancy of the chair, he dropped into it.

For fully five minutes he sat still thinking, reviewing all the circumstances of the peculiar situation upon which the unexpected coming of George Carlyon had broken.

He asked himself whether he was really in love with the fair Madge, and whether he would have proposed to her if her cousin had not so unexpectedly turned up? He made no definite reply to his own questioning, but turned to his mail.

The telegram he had opened at once on its receipt. He turned now to the letters. He had opened all but two. The last one was addressed in a woman's handwriting. Breaking the envelope, he took out the letter, and turned first to the signature on the fourth page.

"Millicent Joyce," he read. "Millicent Joyce?" he repeated. Unconsciously he had laid his emphasis on the "Millicent," and he forgot the "Joyce."

But suddenly it came to him that the letter was from Mrs. Joyce, the woman whom he had helped to save from drowning on the night of that memorable day when the great chance of his life had come to him.

"Poor soul!" he muttered. "I wonder what she has written about?" The next instant he was reading the letter.

Tom Hammond cast his eyes over the letter which Mrs. Joyce had sent him, and which ran thus:

"Dear Sir,

"I gave you my word that if ever I was in special trouble or need I would write, or come to you for help.

"I did not promise you, however, that if any great joy or blessing should come to me, that I would let you know. I don't think I believed any joy could ever possibly come into my life again. But joy and wondrous gladness have come into my life, and in an altogether unexpected way.

"You will remember how I said to you in parting, that morning, that your strong, cheery words had given me a clearer view of God than any sermon I had ever listened to. That impression deepened rather than diminished when I got home. My husband, I heard, had been sent to Wandsworth Prison for a month, for assaulting the police when drunk.

"And in this month of quiet from his brutalities, the great joy of my life came to me. I began to attend religious services from the very first night after my return home. I went to church, chapel, mission hall, and Salvation Army.

"One night I went to the hall of the Mission for Railway Men. A lady was speaking that night, and God found me, and saved me. All that I had ever heard from my dear father's lips, when he preached about conversion, came back to me, and that night I passed from death to life.

"The subject of the address was 'The Coming of the Lord.' I listened in amazement as the lady speaker declared that, for this age, God evidently meant that this truth of the near coming of Christ should have almost, if not quite, the most prominent place in all public preaching.

"I was startled to hear her say that there were nearly three hundred direct references to the second coming of Christ in the Gospels and Epistles, and that there were thus more than double the number of references to that subject than even to that of salvation through the blood of the Atonement.

"With her Bible in her hand, she turned readily to a score of passages as illustrations of her statement, and all through her address she never made a statement without backing it up by Scripture. One thing she said laid a tremendous grip upon me, and led me to an immediate decision for Christ: she said, 'How often is the possibility of sudden death advanced by a preacher as an incentive to unsaved souls to yield to God!

"But how poor an argument is that compared with the near approach of Christ! Sudden death might come to one person in a congregation before twenty-four hours, but in a sense, that would touch that one person only. But if Christ came to take up His people from the earth —the dead in Christ from their graves, the living from their occupations, etc.,—this would affect every unsaved soul in every part of the country, of the world, even.'"

Tom Hammond paused in his reading.

"What on earth can she mean?" he murmured, under his breath. Then he went on from the letter:

"I gave myself up to God there and then, Mr. Hammond, and am seeking now to live so that, should Christ come, even before I finish this letter, I may be ready to be caught up to meet Him in the air."

Hammond paused again.

"What can the woman mean?" he murmured again. With the letter held in his hand, his eyes became fixed upon space, his mind was searching for something that he had recently heard or read bearing on this strange topic. The clue seemed almost within grasp, yet for awhile he could not recall it.

Suddenly it came to him. A volume of poems had been sent to him for review, amid the excitement of the second day's issue of "The Courier." He had glanced rapidly through the book, had written a brief line for his paper, acknowledging the receipt of the book, and promising to refer to it fully at some later date.

"That book," he mused, "had something in it about—about——"

He got up from the rocker, took his place at his table, then wheeled about slowly in his revolving chair, and began searching his book-case. In an instant his keen eye picked out the volume he sought. He wheeled round again to his table, the book in his hand.

He turned a moment to the title-page. "Ezekiel and Other Poems," he read. "By B. M."

"B. M.," he mused, "Whom have I heard writes under those initials? Ah! I rember! Mrs. Miller —Barbara Miller."

He ran the gilt-edged leaves rapidly through his practised fingers, his quick eye catching enough of the running pages to satisfy him. Suddenly he paused in his search. His eye had lit upon what he sought, and he began to read:

"COMING."

"At even, or at midnight, or at the cock-crowing, or in the morning."

"It may be in the evening,
  When the work of the day is done,
And you have time to sit in the twilight
  And watch the sinking sun,
While the long, bright day dies slowly
  Over the sea,
And the hour grows quiet and holy
  With thoughts of Me;
While you hear the village children
  Passing along the street,
Among those thronging footsteps
  May come the sound of My feet.

"Therefore I tell you, 'Watch,'
  By the light of the evening star,
When the room is growing dusky
  As the clouds afar;
Let the door be on the latch
  In your home,
For it may be through the gloaming
  I will come."

He paused in his reading for a moment, for, like a voice near by, the drone of that blind beggar's reading came to him, as he had heard it that day on the embankment.

"This same Jesus shall so come in like manner as ye have seen Him go."

"I remember," he mused, "how that sentence arrested me. My mind was utterly pre-occupied a moment before, but that wondrous sentence pierced my pre-occupation."

His eyes dropped to the poem again, and he read on :—

> "It may be when midnight
>   Is heavy on the land,
> And the black waves lying dumbly
>   Along the sand ;
> When the moonless night draws close,
> And the lights are out in the house ;
> When the fires burn low and red,
> And the watch is ticking loudly
>   Beside the bed.
> Though you sleep, tired out, on your couch,
> Still your heart must wake and watch
> In the dark room ;
> For it may be that at midnight
>   I will come."

He read rapidly, but more eagerly interested each moment. The next section he scarcely paused upon, but the fourth he lingered over, and then read it the second time :

> "It may be in the morning,
>   When the sun is bright and strong,
> And the dew is glittering sharply
>   Over the little lawn ;
> When the waves are laughing loudly
>   Along the shore,
> And the little birds sing sweetly
>   About the door ;
> With the long day's work before you,
>   You rise up with the sun

And the neighbours come in to talk a little
   Of all that must be done:
But remember that I may be the next
   To come in at the door,
To call you from your busy work
   For evermore.
As you work, your heart must watch,
For the door is on the latch
   In your room,
And it may be in the morning
   I will come."

He read on with a strange, breathless interest the
next two pages of poem, then, with a sudden sense of
hush upon him, he went carefully over the concluding
lines:

"So I am watching quietly
   Every day.
Whenever the sun shines brightly,
   I rise and say,
'Surely it is the shining of His face!"
And look unto the gates of His high place
   Beyond the sea,
For I know He is coming shortly
   To summon me.
And when a shadow falls across the window
   Of my room,
Where I am working my appointed task,
I lift my head to watch the door, and ask
   If He is come;
And the angel answers sweetly
   In my home:
'Only a few more shadows,
   And He will come.'"

The face of Tom Hammond, as he laid down the book,
was full of a strange, new perplexity. "Strange, very!"
he muttered. "Do you know Joyce, Mr. Simpson?" Hammond asked a reporter. "He used to be on the staff
of the——"

"'Daily Tatler,'" cried the man. "Knew him well
years ago, sir. Old school-fellows, in fact. Got wrong

with the drink, sir. Gone to the dogs, and——"

"Have you seen or heard anything of him this last month, Mr. Simpson?"

"Yes, sir. He's grown worse than ever. Magistrate at Bow Street, committing him for three days, said fellow ought to be put in Broadmoor. Pity his poor wife, sir. Perfect lady, sir."

"You know Mrs. Joyce, then?" Hammond queried.

The reporter sighed, "Rather, sir! Wished a thousand times I could have had her for a wife, and he'd had mine. I should have had a happier life. And he——"

The man laughed grimly. "Well, he'd have had a tartar!"

Hammond had heard something about the shrewish wife Simpson had unfortunately married. But he had learned all he wanted to know, so dismissed the poor, ill-married fellow.

"I think I must call upon Mrs. Joyce, and learn more about this strange matter of the coming Christ," he told himself.

He copied the address from the head of the letter into his pocket-book, then turned to the last letter of his mail.

This proved to be a comparatively short letter, but, to Hammond, a deeply-interesting one. It was signed "Abraham Cohen," and the writer explained that he was a Jew, who had taken the "Courier" from the very first number, and had not only become profoundly interested in the recent utterances of the editor in the "Prophet's Chamber" column, but he had, for some days, been impressed with the desire to write to the "Prophet."

"Will you pardon me, sir," the letter went on, "if I

say that it would be to your immense advantage, now that your mind has become aroused to the facts and history of our race, if you would get in touch with some really well-read, intelligent Jew who knows our people well, knows their history, past, present, and future, as far as the latter can be known from our Scriptures and sacred books. Should you care to fall in with my suggestion, I should be pleased to supply you with the names and addresses of several good and clever men of our people.

"Yours obediently,

"ABRAHAM COHEN."

As he folded the letter slowly, Hammond told himself that there was something in the letter that drew him towards the writer.

"I will hunt him up, for it is evident that he is as enthusiastic over his people's history as he is intelligent. I will see what to-morrow brings. Now to work."

He put Cohen's letter in his pocket, and turned to the hundred and one editorial claims upon his time.

CHAPTER VIII.

REVERIE.

IN spite of the time of the year, the evening was almost as warm as one in June. Madge Finisterre was on one of the wide hotel balconies overlooking the Embankment. She had dined with her cousin, George Carlyon, but instead of going out of town that evening with him—he had pressed her strongly to go,—she had elected to spend a quiet evening alone.

London's roar, subdued a little, it is true, at that hour, rose all around her where she sat. The cup of coffee she had brought to her, cooled where it stood upon the little table at her elbow. She had forgotten it.

Her mind was engrossed with the memory of the latter part—the interrupted part—of that interview with Tom Hammond that afternoon.

"What would have happened if George Carlyon had not turned up at that moment?" she mused,—"if we had been left alone and undisturbed another five minutes?"

Her cheeks burned as she whispered softly to herself:

"I believe Tom Hammond would have proposed to me. If he had, what should I have replied?"

A far-away look crept into her eyes. She was back again in the little town where she had been "reared," as she herself would have said. We have many villages in England larger, more populous, more busy, than her "town," but, then, the people of her land talk "big."

Before her mind's eye there rose the picture of her

father's store, a huge, rambling concern built of wood, with a frontage of a hundred feet, and a colonnade of turned wooden pillars that supported a verandah that ran the whole length.

Every item of the interior of the store came vividly before her mind, the very odour of the place—a curious blend of groceries, drapery, rope, oils and colours, tobacco,—seemed suddenly to fill her nostrils. And in that instant, though she scarcely realized it, the first real touch of nostalgia came to her.

She saw the postal section of the store littered with men, all smoking, most of them yarning. One after another dropped in, and, with a "Howdy, all?" dropped upon a coil of white cotton rope, or lounged against a counter or cask. "Dollars" and "cents" floated in speech all around, while the men waited for the mail. It was late that night.

A week before she had sailed for England, she had gone down to the store, as she had gone every evening about mail-time, and, entering at the end nearest her home, she had come upon the scene that had now so suddenly risen before her mind's eye. She had traversed all the narrow alley-way between the stored-up supplies, from which the various departments were stocked, singing as she went:

> "The world is circumbendibus,
>   We're all going round;
> We have a try to fly the sky,
>   But still we're on the ground.
> We every one go round the sun,
>   We're moving night and day;
> And milkmen all go round the run
>   Upon their Milky Way."

"We're all circumbendibus,
    Wherever we may be,
We're all circumbendibus,
    On land or on sea.
Rich or poor or middling,
    Wherever we are found,
We're all circumbendibus,
    We're all going round."

She had punctuated the chorus with a series of jerked
steps, her high heels striking the wooden floor in a kind
of castanet accompaniment. Every waiting man had
risen to his feet as she came upon them in that post-office
section, and she had answered their rising with a military
salute.

In the great mirror that ran from floor to ceiling of
the store, she had caught a glimpse of herself. She
recalled, even now, exactly what she was wearing that
evening—a white muslin frock, a very wide sash of rich
silk—crushed strawberry colour—about her waist, the
long ends of the sash floating behind her almost to the
high heels of her dainty bronze shoes. A knot of the
same-hued ribbon, narrow, of course, with streamers
flying, was fastened at her left shoulder. Her wide-brimmed hat was trimmed with the same colour. She had
known that she made a handsome picture before she read
the light of admiration in the eyes of the post-office
loungers.

"Have you heard the news, boys?" she asked.

"Aw, guess we hev, Miss Madge."

It was Ulysses Fletcher who had acted as spokesman.

In some surprise, and not altogether pleased, she had
wheeled sharply round to the lantern-jawed Ulysses
and asked,

"How did you hear the news, Ulysses? Dad didn't

tell you, I'm sure, for he promised me I should tell you all myself."

"Met a coon down to the depot, an' I guess he wur chuck full o' it, an' 'e ups an' tells me."

"A coon told you?" she had cried in ever-increasing amazement.

"Sartin, Miss Madge!"

"A coon!" she had repeated. "A coon—told you—down at the depot—that—I was—going—to Europe next week!"

Every eye had stared in wondering astonishment at Madge Finisterre at her announcement that she was going to Europe. Then there was a general laugh, and one of the smartest of the "boys" had cried:—

"I low there's been a mistake some, Miss Madge, an' that, too, all roun'. Fact is, we've been runnin' two separate tickets over this news business, an' thought it wur one an' the same. We wur talkin' 'bout Seth Hammond's herd o' hogs as wur cut up by the Poughkeepsie express 'smarnin'."

She had joined in the laugh, and then in reply to the question of another of the men, as to whether it was really true that she was going to "Urop," she had replied in the affirmative, adding, by way of explanation:

"I guess you all know that my momma is British, that she belonged to what the Britishers call, 'the Quality. She was the youngest sister of Sir Archibald Carlyon, was travelling over here, out west, when she was about my age, got fixed up in an awkward shop by half-breeds, and was rescued by my dear old poppa. Fact, that's how he came to be my poppa, for she married him. Spite of her high connections in England, she was very poor, and she loved dad. If dear momma could only face the water journey, she'd go over with me."

"Air you goin' alone, Miss?" one of the boys had asked.

Then—how well she remembered it to-night!—she had given the answer, part of which she had given to George Carlyon that very day:

"Oh, I'll git all right, boys, you can bet on that, without anyone dandying around me. For I guess if there's one thing the Britishers are learning about our women, it's this—that if a United States gel's got dollars under her boots to wheel around on it ain't much fuss for her to skate through their old country, nor yet through Europe, come to that, even if she has no more language under her tongue than good, plain, Duchess county American."

With a merry smile, for which there had been no scrambling, since it was shed upon them all, she had passed on to where she knew she would find her father, ringing her boot-heels, castanet fashion, as she sang lightly:

> "Mary's gone wid a coon,
> Mary's gone wid a coon;
> Dere's heaps o' trubble on de ole man's min'
> Since Mary flit wid de coon."

How vividly it all came up before her in this hour of quiet reverie! But her mind flitted swiftly to another scene, one that had been hanging in the background of all her thought ever since (thinking of Tom Hammond and the interrupted conversation,) she had been reminded of home and its happenings.

There had been a Donation Party for their pastor (Episcopalian Methodist) at the house of one of the members on the very night of the store scene. Madge ad gone, of course. Balhang was wont to say that Donation Party simply could not be run without her.

Sitting on that Embankment hotel balcony, with eyes xed on the lamps, the river, the bridge, the traffic yet eeing nothing of it all, that Donation Party all came ack to her. Things had been a bit stiff and formal at rst, as they often are at such gatherings.

The adults sat around and talked on current topics –how much turkeys would fetch for Thanksgiving, vhether it would pay best to sell them plucked or nplucked, what would folks do for cranberries for 'hanksgiving, since the cranberry crop had failed that ear—"An' turkey wi'out cranberry ain't wuth a twist ' the tongue."

"An' squash," suggested one old man. "What's turkey vi'out squash? I'd most so soon hev only Boston" i. e., pork and beans) "fur dinner as ter go wi'out quash wi' turkey."

The young folk had been "moping around" like drag-led chickens on a wet day when the barn-door is shut. 'hen, at this juncture, Madge had burst upon the scene. 'he swam into the largest room, swirling round and ound with a kind of waltz movement, to the accom-animent of her own gay voice as she sang:

> "I said, 'My dear, I'm glad!'
> Said she, 'I'm glad you're glad!'
> Said I, 'I'm glad you're glad I'm glad,
> It is so very, very nice;
> It makes it seem worth twice the price,
> So glad you're glad I'm glad!'"

With a gay laugh she had turned to the hostess, aying;

"Things want hustling a bit here, Miss Julie. Everyone is as glum as a whip-poor-will that is fixed up with the grippe."

In the quiet of that corner of the hotel balcony she smiled at these remembrances of her nonsense that night. She had started the young people playing their favourite games of "Whisper," "Amsterdam," etc., in two or three of the smaller rooms; then had raced away again to the room where the adults were sitting squarely against the wall, as grim as "brazen images." Dropping on to the piano stool, she struck a few soft, tender notes, suggestive of some very gracious hymn, then suddenly broke into song:

> "Oh, dat's so! Oh, dat's so!
> Dar is nuffing 'neath de moon dat'll satisfy dis coon.
> Like a K—I—double S, kiss,
> Since dat Cupid, wid his dart, made a keyhole in my heart
> For dat M—I—double S, miss."

Behind a corner of the curtain the young pastor had watched and listened. He had thought his presence unknown to her. He was mistaken.

For three-quarters of an hour she had been the life of that room. Then, suddenly, as she was singing at the piano, the room grew very quiet. She was aroused by a voice just behind her ear, saying:

"Miss Finisterre, are you going to supper with this first batch, or will you wait the next turn?"

Turning, she found herself face to face with the young pastor, the room being otherwise empty. His gaze was very warm, very ardent. She had flushed under the power of that gaze.

She had railed him on his extra seriousness, and he had answered,

"Don't, Madge! you must know why I am grave and sad, to-night." (He had never called her Madge before.)

"No, I don't," she had replied.

"In less than a week," he went on, "so I have heard to-night, you leave Balhang. You are going to Europe, and will be away long months, perhaps a year."

She had gazed at him in honest wonder, not fully grasping his meaning.

"Why," she asked, "should that make you sad?"

He had leaned closer towards her. There was no one to see them. The heavy door-curtain had slipped from its hook, and shut them in. Where her hand rested on the rounded, polished arm of the piano, his larger hand had moved, and her white fingers were clasped in his larger ones. His eyes had sought hers, and, under the hypnotic power of the strong love in his eyes, she had been compelled to meet his gaze.

"I thought, dear, you must have seen how, for a long time, I had learned to love you, Madge."

His clasp on her fingers had tightened. He had leaned nearer to her still. No man's face, save her father's had ever been so close to hers before, and the contact strangely affected her. She felt the warmth of his breath, the heat of his clean, wholesome flesh; even the scent of the soap he had used—or was is some perfume in his clothing?—filled all her sense of smell.

The perfume was violet, and she remembered tonight how, for many a day, she could not smell violets without recalling that moment, and seeing again the strong, earnest, eager face, with the fire of a mighty love burning in the eyes.

To-night she heard again the yearning, pleading voice

as he had cried: "Madge, Madge, my darling! Can you ever guess how great is my love for you? Tell me, dear, do you, can you, love me in return? Will you be my wife? Will you come into all my life to bless it? And let me be wholly yours to help, to bless, to strengthen, to love, to cherish you? Tell me, darling!"

And she had cried, almost piteously:

"I don't know how to answer you, pastor. It is all so sudden. I knew, of course, that we were great friends, and I am sure I like you very much, but—this proposal! Why, I never dreamed that you cared for me like that, for how could I be a minister's wife? I am such a gay, thoughtless, foolish little thing—I——"

There had followed more tender pleading, and she had finally said, "If you love me, Homer, as you say you do, please do not bother me any more now. Wait until I come back from Europe—then—then——"

"What, Madge?" he had cried softly, eagerly.

"If I can honestly say 'Yes,'" she had replied, "I will and I will not even wait for you to ask me again."

He had bent over her. His gaze held her fascinated. She thought he was going to take toll of her lips before his right was confirmed. But at that instant there had come a rush of feet, a sound of many voices. The curtain was flung aside, just as her fingers strayed over the keys of the instrument, and the pastor succeeded in regaining his old unseen nook.

"I guess Miss Julie's waitin' fur yer, Miss Madge, ter go ter yer supper," bawled an old deacon of the church.

She had swept the ivory keys with rollicking touch, and sang in gayest style:

> "Allow me to say Ta-ta!
> I bid you good-day. Ta-ta!
> I wish I could stay,
> But I'm going away.
> Allow me to say Ta-ta!"

Amid the uproarious laughter of everyone in the room, she had bounded away to supper.

Except for one moment, when she was leaving the house for home, and he had helped her on with her cloak, the pastor had not spoken again directly to her that evening. He had managed then to whisper,

"God bless you, my darling! I shall pray for you, and live on the hope I read in your eyes to-night."

It was all this which had risen so strangely before her mind, as to-night, on that hotel balcony, she had begun to ask herself how much she really cared for Tom Hammond, and what answer she would have given him had he proposed to her that afternoon.

"I told pastor," she murmured, "that night, that I was not sure of myself. I am no nearer being sure of myself now than I was then."

The scene with Hammond rose up before her, and she added: "I am less sure, I think, than ever!"

She gazed fixedly where the double line of lamps gleamed on the near-distant bridge. For a moment she tried to compare the two lives—that of an American Methodist pastor's wife, with endless possibilities of doing good, and that of the wife of a comparatively wealthy newspaper editor-manager.

"Should I like to marry a popular man?" she asked herself. "I read somewhere once that popular men. like popular actors, make bad husbands, that they cannot endure the tameness of an audience of one."

She laughed low, and a little amusedly, as she added,

"Oh, well, Tom Hammond has not asked me to marry him. Perhaps he never will—and—well, 'sufficient for the day is the evil thereof.' Pastor once preached from that, I remember."

The night had grown cooler. She shivered a little as she rose and passed into the lighted room beyond.

Two hours later, as she laid her head upon the pillow, she murmured, "I don't see how I could marry the pastor! Why, I haven't 'got religion' yet. I am not 'converted,' as these Britishers would say!"

CHAPTER IX.

A THREAT.

TOM HAMMOND paused before the house that bore the number at the head of Mrs. Joyce's letter. It was in a mean street, and his soul went out in pity towards the unfortunate woman, who, with all her refinement, was compelled to live amid such squalid surroundings.

"And heart-starved, too," he mused, pityingly. "Heart-starved for the want of love, of sympathy, of the sense of soul-union that makes life with a married partner at all bearable."

"Yus, sir; Mrs. Joss lives yere. Top floor, lef' 'and side. Yer kin go hup!"

A child had opened the door in response to his knock. Following the directions given, Tom Hammond climbed the dirty stairs. On the top landing were two doors. The one on the right was fast shut; that on the left was ajar a few inches. His approach did not seem to have been heard. Mrs. Joyce, the only occupant of the room, was seated at a bare deal table, sewing briskly.

He stretched out his hand to tap at the door, but some impulse checked him for a moment. He had the opportunity to observe her closely, and he did so.

She sat facing the window; the light shone full upon her. She was dressed in a well-worn but well-fitting black gown. Round her throat—how pure and white the skin was!—she wore a white turnover collar, like a nurse, white cuffs at her wrists completing the nurse idea.

Her hair—she had loosened it earlier because of a slight headache—hung in clustering waves on her neck, and was held back behind her ears with a comb on either side. There was a rare softness and refinement in the pale face that drooped over her sewing. Seen as Tom Hammond saw her then, Mrs. Joyce was a really beautiful woman.

He gazed for a few moments at the picture, amazed at the rapidity of her sewing movements.

"The tragedy of Tom Hood's 'Song of the Shirt,'" he muttered, as he watched the gleam of the flying needle.

> "Oh, men with sisters dear!
>   Oh, men with mothers and wives!
> It is not linen you're wearing out,
>   But human creature's lives!
>   Stitch, stitch, stitch,
>   In poverty, hunger, and dirt,
> Sewing at once, with a double thread,
>   A shroud as well as a shirt."

Under the magnetic constraint of his fixed gaze the woman looked towards the door. She recognized her visitor, and with a little glad cry started to her feet. Tom Hammond pushed the door open and entered the room. She sprang to meet him.

Now that he saw her, he realized the expression of her face had changed. Heaven—all the heaven of God's indwelling pardon, love, peace, had come to dwell with her. All that she had said in her letter of her new-found joy, was fully confirmed by her looks.

"How good of you to come to see me, Mr. Hammond!" she cried, as she felt the clasp of his hand.

"How good of you to write me of your new-found happiness!" He smiled back into her glad, eager eyes.

He took the chair she offered, and with a question or two sought to lead her on to talk of the subject about which he had come to see her.

"The very title of the subject," Hammond explained, "is perfectly foreign to me."

"It was all so, *so* foreign to me," she returned. Then, as swift tears flooded her eyes, she turned to him with a little rapturous cry, saying,—

"And it would all have been foreign to me for ever, but for *you*, Mr. Hammond. I never, *never* can forget that but for you my soul would have been in a suicide's hell, where hope and mercy could never have reached me. As long as I shall live I shall never forget the awful rush of soul-accusation that swept over me, when my body touched the foul waters of that muddy river that night. The chill and shock of the waters I did *not* feel, but the chill of eternal condemnation for my madness and sin I did feel.

"I saw all my life as in a flash. All the gracious warnings and pleadings that ever, in my hearing, fell from my sainted father's lips, as he besought men and women to be reconciled to God, seemed to swoop down upon me, condemning me for my unbelief and sin. Then—then you came to my rescue—and———"

Her tears were dropping thick and fast now.

"And—my soul—had respite given in which to—to—seek God—because—you saved my body."

Overcome with her emotion, she turned her head to wipe away the grateful tears. When next she faced him, her voice was low and tender, her eyes glowed with a light that Tom Hammond had never seen in a human face before.

"Now, if my Lord come," she said softly, rapturously, "whether at morning, at noontide, at midnight, or cock-crowing, I shall be ready to meet Him in the air.

"I used to think that if ever I was converted, I should meet my dear father and mother at the last day, at the great final end of all things.

"But now I know that if Jesus came for His people to-day, that I should meet my dear ones to-day. For when 'the Lord Himself shall descend from heaven . . . the dead in Christ shall rise first: then we which are alive and remain shall be caught up together with them in the clouds, to meet the Lord in the air: and so shall we ever be with the Lord.'"

Tom Hammond gazed at the speaker in wonder. The glory that filled her face, the triumph and rapture that rang in her voice, were a strange revelation to him.

"A starvation wage for making slop-shirts," he mused, "yet more than triumphing over every discomfort of poverty by the force of the divine hope that dominates her! What is this hope?"

"Tell me of this wondrous thing, Mrs. Joyce," he said, aloud, "that can transmute your poverty and suffering to triumph and rapture, and your comfortless garret to a heaven on earth."

"Before I begin," she replied, "tell me, Mr. Hammond, have ever you seen this?"

From the window-shelf she reached a tiny envelope booklet.

"'Long Odds'!" he said, reading the boldly-printed title of the book. "No; I have never seen this. It sounds sporting, rather."

"Take it, Mr. Hammond," she went on; "if it does nothing else, it will awaken your interest in this wonderful subject."

He slipped the book into his breast-pocket. She opened her mouth to speak again, when a sound from outside caught her ear. She started to her feet; her face turned deadly pale. The next instant the door was flung noisily open, and her husband entered the room.

The blear-eyed, drunken scoundrel glared at the two seated figures, then laughed evilly as he cried,—

"Turned religious? Oho! oho! Like all the rest of your religious people, make a mantle—a regular down-to-your-feet ulster—of your religion to cover every blackness and filthiness of life."

"Silence, you foul-mouthed blackguard!"

Tom Hammond's lips were white with the indignation that filled him, as he flung his command to the man.

"Silence yourself, Tom Hammond!" bellowed the drunken scoundrel. "I know you," he went on. "You're a big bug now! Think no end of yourself, and of your messing paper. Perhaps you'll say you came to invite me to join your staff, now that I've caught you here?"

His sneering tone changed to one of bitterest hate, as he turned to the white, trembling woman.

"You're a beauty, ain't you? Profess to turn saint; then, when you think I'm clear away, you receive visits from fine gentlemen! Gentlemen? bah! they're——"

"Silence, you drunken, foul-mouthed beast!" again interrupted Tom Hammond.

There was something amazing in the command that rang in the indignant tones of his voice.

"Unless," he went on, "you want to find yourself in the grip of the law."

For a moment or two Joyce was utterly cowed! then the devil in him reared its head again, and he hissed,

"You clear out of here, and remember this; if I have to keep sober for a year to do it, I'll ruin you Tom Hammond, I will!"

He laughed with an almost demoniacal glee, as he went on:

"I can write a par yet, you know. I'll dip my pen in the acid of hate—hate, the hate of devils, my beauty—and then get Fletcher to put them into his paper. He's not in love with the 'Courier,' or with Tom Hammond, the Editor."

"You scurrilous wretch!" It was all that Hammond deigned to reply.

"Good day, Mrs. Joyce!" he bowed to the white-faced woman.

For her sake he did not offer to shake hands, but moved away down the stairs.

He caught a hansom a few moments after leaving the mean street. He had purposed, when he started out that morning, to hunt up his other correspondent, the Jew, Abraham Cohen. But after the scene he had just witnessed, he felt quite unwilling to interview a stranger.

"I wish," he mused, as he sat back in the hansom, "I had not gone near that poor soul. I am afraid my visit may make it awkward for her."

His eyes darkened as he added: "And even for myself. It will be very awkward if that drunken brute puts his threat into execution—and he *will*, I believe. Innuendo is a glass stiletto, which, driven into the victim's character, into his heart and then snapped off from the hilt, leaves no clue to the striker of the blow. And a demon like that Joyce, playing into the hands of a cur like Fletcher, may slay a fellow by a printed innuendo, and yet the pair may easily keep outside the reach of the law of libel."

For the first time since the floating of the "Courier;" his spirits became clouded.

"Then, too," he muttered, "there is this sudden breakdown of Marsden, and, for the life of me, I don't know where to look for a fellow, whom I could secure at short notice, who is at all fit for the 'Courier's' *second*."

His face had grown moody. His eyes were full of an unwonted depression.

"If only," he went on, "Bastin had been in England, and were to be got——" He sighed. There was perplexity in the sigh.

"Where on earth can Ralph be all these years?" he muttered.

He glanced out of the cab to ascertain his own whereabouts. In two minutes more he would be at the office.

CHAPTER X

IN THE NICK OF TIME.

AS Tom Hammond's cab drew up at the office, another hansom drew up a yard ahead of his. The occupant alighted at the same instant as did Hammond, and glanced in his direction. Both men leaped forward, their hands were clasped in a grip that told of a very warm friendship. Like simultaneous pistol shots there leaped from their separate lips,—

"Tom Hammond!"

"Ralph Bastin?"

The friends presently passed into the great building, arm linked in arm, laughing and talking like holiday school-boys.

"Not three minutes ago, as I drove along in my cab, I was saying, 'Oh! if only I could lay my hand on Ralph!'"

They were seated by this time in Tom Hammond's room.

"Why? What did you want, Tom—anything special?" the bronzed, travelled Bastin asked.

"Rather, Ralph! My second, poor Frank Marsden, has broken down suddenly; it's serious, may even prove fatal, the doctors say. Anyway, he won't be fit (if he recovers at all) for a year or more."

He leaned eagerly towards his friend as he spoke, and asked,

"Are you open to lay hold of the post?"

"Yes."

"When?"

"To-morrow, if you like !"

"Good !"

Hammond stretched his hand out. Bastin grasped it. Then they talked over terms, duties, etc.

"But you, man?" said Hammond, when the last bit of shop had been talked. "Where have you been? What have you been doing?"

"Busy for an hour, Tom?" Bastin asked, by way of reply.

"No!"

"Come round to my diggings, then; not far—Blooms-bury. We can talk as we go. I shall have time to give you a skeleton of my adventures, to be filled in later. Then, when we get to my hang-out, I can tell you, when you have seen *her*, the story of my chief adventure, for it concerns her."

Hammond flashed a quick, wondering glance at his friend.

"*Her!*" he said; "are you married, then?"

"No," laughed Bastin, "but I've adopted a child. But come on, man !"

The pair left the office. In the cab, talking very rapidly, Bastin gave the skeleton sketch of his wander-ings, but saying no word of the promised great adventure.

Tom Hammond never forgot the first sight of his friend's adopted child. There was a low grate in the room, a blazing fire of leaping, flaming coals in the grate. Curled up in a deep saddle-bag arm-chair was the loveliest girl-child Hammond had ever seen.

She must have been half asleep, or in a deep reverie, but as the two men advanced into the room she sprang from the chair, and, with eyes gleaming with delight, bounded to meet Bastin. Wreathing her arms about his neck, she crooned softly over him some tongue of her own.

She was loveliness incarnated. Her eyes, black as sloes, were big, round, and wide in their staring wonder at Hammond's appearance. Her hair was a mass of short curls. She was dark of skin as some Spanish beauty.

Her costume lent extra charm to her appearance; for she wore a long, Grecian-like robe of some light, diaphanous ivory-cream fabric, engirdled at the waist with a belt composed of some sort of glistening peacock-green shells, buckled with frosted silver. The simple but exquisite garment had only short shoulder-sleeves, and was cut low round the throat and neck, and finished there —as were the edges of the shoulder-sleeves—with a two-inch wide band of sheeny silk of the same colour as the shells of her belt. The opening at the neck of the robe was fastened with a brooch of frosted silver of the same pattern, only smaller, as the buckle of the belt.

From beneath the silk-bound hem of her robe there peeped bronze slippers, encasing the dantiest little crimsoned-stockinged feet ever used for pedalling this rough old earth's crust.

Bastin introduced the child. She gave Tom her hand, and lifted her wondrous eyes to his, answering his question as to her health in the prettiest of broken English he had ever heard.

A moment or two later the three friends were seated —Tom and Bastin in armchairs opposite each other, the child (Viola, Bastin had christened her) on a low stool between Bastin's knees.

"Shall we use the old lingo—French?" Bastin asked

the question in the Bohemian Parisian they had been wont to use together years before.

"As you please, Ralph," Hammond replied.

"I have told you hurriedly something of where I have been," Bastin began. "But I have reserved my *great* story until I could tell it to you here——" He glanced down at the child at his feet. "I heard," he went on, "when at La Caribe—as everyone hears who stays long in the place—that each year, in spite of the laws of the whites, who are in power, a child is sacrificed to the Carib deities, and I longed to know if it were true.

"During my first few week's sojourn on the little island of Utilla, I was able to render one of the old priests a service, which somehow became so exaggerated in his eyes that there was almost literally nothing that he would not do for me, and eventually he yielded to my entreaties to give me a chance to see for myself the yearly sacrifice, which was due in a month's time.

"During that month of waiting I made many sketches of this wonderful neighbourhood, and became acquainted with this little Carib maiden, painting her in three or four different ways. The child became intensely attached to me, and I to her, and we were always together in the daytime.

"As the time drew near for the sacrifice I noticed that the little one grew very elated, and there was a new flash in her eyes, a kind of rapturous pride. I asked her no question as to this change, putting it down as girlish pride in being painted by the 'white prince,' as she insisted on calling me.

"I need not trouble you, my dear fellow, with unnecessary details of how and where the old priest led me on the eventful night, which was a black as Erebus, but come to the point where the real interest begins.

"It was midnight when at last I had been smuggled into that mysterious cave, which, if only a tithe of what is reported be half true, has been damned by some of the awfullest deeds ever perpetrated. My priest-guide had made me swear, before starting, that whatever I saw I would make no sign, utter no sound, telling me that if I did, and we were discovered, we should both be murdered there and then.

"We had hardly hidden ourselves before the whole centre of the cave became illuminated with a mauve-coloured flame that burned up from a flat brass brazier, and seemed like the coloured fires used in pantomime effects on the English stage. By this wonderful light I saw a hundred and fifty or more Carib men and women file silently into the cave, and take up their positions in orderly rows all round the place. When they had all mustered, a sharp note was struck upon the carimba, a curious one-stringed instrument, and the circles of silent savages, dropped into squatting position on their heels. Then the weirdest of all weird music began, the instruments being a drum, a flute, and the carimba.

"But my whole attention became absorbed by the grouping in the centre of the room—the fire-dish had been shifted to one side, and I saw a hideous statue, squatted on a rudely-constructed, massive table, the carved hands gripping a bowl that rested on the stone knees of the image. The head of the hideous god was encircled with a very curious band, that looked, from where I stood, like bead and grass and feather work. The face—cheeks and forehead—was scored with black, green and red paint, the symbolic colours of that wondrous race that once filled all Central America.

"In the back part of the wide, saucer-like edge of the bowl which rested on the knees of the statue, there burned a light-blue flame, and whether it was from this fire, or from the larger one that burned in the wide, shallow brazier on the floor, I cannot positively say, but a lovely fragrance was diffused from one or the other.

"Before this strange altar stood three very old priests, while seven women (sukias,) as grizzled as the men, stood at stated intervals about the altar. One of these hideous hags had a dove in her hand; another held a young kid clasped between her strong brown feet; a third held the sacrificial knife, a murderous-looking thing, made of volcano glass, short in blade, and with a peculiar jagged kind of edge; another of these hags grasped a snake by the neck—a blood-curdling-looking tamagas, a snake as deadly as a rattle-snake.

"Opposite the centre-man of the three old priests stood a girl-child, about ten years of age, and perfectly nude. During the first few moments the vapourous kind of smoke that was wafted by a draught somewhere, from the fire-pan on the floor of the cave, hid the child's features, though I could see how beautiful of form she was; then, as the smoke-wreath presently climbed straight up, I was startled to see that the child was my little friend.

"In my amaze I had almost given vent to some exclamation, but my old priest-guide was watching me, and checked me.

"My little one's beautiful head was wreathed with jasmine, and a garland of purple madre-de-cacoa blossoms hung about her lovely shoulders.

"Suddenly, like the barely-audible notes of the opening music of some orchestral number, the voice of one of the priests began to chant; in turn the two other priests took up the strain; then each of the seven hags in their turn, and anon each in the first circle of squatting worshippers, followed by each woman in the second row: and in this order the chant proceeded, until, weird and low, every voice was engaged.

"Suddenly the combined voices ceased, and one woman's voice alone rose upon the stillness; and following the sound of the voice, I saw that it was the mother of my little native child-friend. I had not noticed her before—she had been squatting out of sight. Hers was not the chant of the others, but a strange, mournful wail. It lasted about a minute and a-half; then, rising to her feet, she gently thrust the child forward towards the altar, then laid herself face down on the floor of the cave.

"The little one leaned against the edge of the altar, and taking up, with a tiny pair of bright metal tongs, a little fire out of the back edge of the bowl on the knees of the god, she lighted another fire on the front edge of the bowl, her suddenly-illuminated face filled with a glowing pride.

"Then, at a signal from the head priest, the child lifted her two hands, extended them across the altar, when they were each seized by the two other priests, and the beautiful little body was drawn slowly, gently over, until the smooth breast almost touched the sacrificial fire she had herself lighted.

"Then I saw the woman who had held the knife suddenly yield it up to the head priest, and I made an unconscious movement to spring forward.

"My guide held me, and whispered his warning in my ear: yet, even though I must be murdered myself, I felt I dared not see that sweet young life taken.

"Like a man suffering with nightmare, who wants to move, but cannot, I stood transfixed, fascinated, one instant longer. But in that flashing instant the head priest had swept, with lightning speed, the edge of that hideous knife twice across the little one's breast, and she stood smiling upwards like one hypnotized.

"The priest caught a few drops of the child's blood, and shook them into the bowl of the god; then I saw the little one fall into her mother's arms; there was a second sudden flashing of that hideous knife, a piteous, screaming cry, and I gave vent to a yell—but not *voice* to it,—for the watching guide at my side clapped one hand tightly over my mouth, while with the other he held me from flying out into the ring of devils, whispering in my ear as he held me back,

"'It is the goat that is slain, not the child.'

"Another glance, and I saw that this was so; one flash of that obsidian sacrificial blade across the throat of the kid had been enough, and now the blood was being drained into the bowl of the god.

"I need not detail all the other hideous ceremonies; they lasted for nearly two hours longer, ending with a mad frenzied dance, in which all joined save the priests and the mother and child.

"Every dancer, man and woman, flung off every rag of clothing, and whirled and leaped and gyrated in their perfect nudity, until, utterly exhausted, one after another they sank upon the floor.

"Then slowly they gathered themselves up, reclothed

themselves, and left the cave. And now some large pine torches were lighted, and my guide drew me further back, that the increased glare might not reveal our presence, and I saw the curious ending to this weird night's work. The priests and their seven women sukias opened a pit in the floor of the cave by shifting a great slab of stone, and lowered the idol into the pit. The remains of the kid, the sacrificial knife, and the dove were dropped into the bowl of blood that rested on the knees of the idol; then the sukia that had held the tamagas snake during the whole of those hideous night hours, dropped the writhing thing into the bowl, and the slab was lowered quickly over the pit, every seam around the slab being carefully filled, and the whole thing hidden by sprinkling loose dust and the ashes from the fire over the spot.

"Then, as soon as the last of the performers had cleared the cave, I followed my guide, and with a throbbing head, and full of a sense of strange sickness, I went to the house where I was staying.

"I lay down upon my bed, but could not sleep; and as early as I dared I went round to my little Martarae's home—Martarae was her native name. Her mother met me, said that the child would not come out in the sun to-day, that I might see her for a moment if I pleased, but that she was not very well.

"Sweet little soul! I found her lying on her little bed, with a proud light in her eyes, and a very flushed face.

"A fortnight later the light flesh wounds were healed. She showed me her breast, confided to me the story, and asked me if I did not think she had much to be proud of.

"'Will you keep a secret?' I asked her. She gave me

her promise, and I told her how I had seen the whole thing, and all my fears for her.

"A week later she was orphaned. Her mother was stung by a deadly scorpion, and died in an hour, and I made the child my care.

"She has travelled everywhere with me ever since, and you see how fair and sweet she is, and how beautifully she speaks our English. She is barely twelve, is naturally gifted, and is the very light of my life."

"Would she let me see her breast, Ralph, do you think?" Hammond asked.

Bastin smiled, and spoke a word to the child, and she, rising to her feet and smiling back at him, unfastened the broach at her throat, and, laying back her breast-covering, showed the gleaming, shiny scars. Then as she re-covered her chest, she said softly:

"Ralph has taught me that those gods were evil; but though I shall ever wear this cross in the flesh of my breast, I shall ever love the Christ who died on the world's great cross at Calvary."

"It is a most marvellous story, Ralph," he said tearing his eyes away from the child's clear, searching gaze.

"The more marvellous because absolutely true," returned Bastin.

Then, addressing Viola, and relapsing, of course, into English for her sake, he explained who Tom Hammond was, and that he (Ralph) was going to be associated with him on the same great newspaper.

"Mr. Hammond and you, Viola, must be real good friends," he added.

"Sure, daddy!" the girl said smilingly; "I like him much already——"

She lifted herself slightly until she rested on her knees, and stretching one hand across the hearthrug to Tom Hammond, she laid the other in her guardian's, as she went on:

"Mr. Hammond is good! I know, I know, for his eyes shine true."

A ripple of merry laughter escaped her, as she gazed back into her guardian's face, and added:

"But you, daddy, are always first."

CHAPTER XI.

"LONG ODDS."

FOR a wonder, Tom Hammond could not sleep. Usually, when the last thing had been done, and he was assured that everything was in perfect train for the morning's issue, he ate a small basin of boiled milk and bread, which he invariably took by way of a "nightcap," then went to bed, and slept like a tired ploughman. But to-night slumber would have none of him.

"It must be the various excitements of the day," he muttered. "That story of Ralph's Caribbean child was enough to keep a fellow's brain working for a week. Then there was meeting Ralph so unexpectedly, just, too, when I so lusted for his presence and help. Then there was that Joyce item——"

His mind trailed off to the scene of the morning, every item of it starting up in a new and vivid light. Suddenly he recalled the booklet Mrs. Joyce had given him.

"I can't sleep," he murmured; "I'll find that thing and read it."

His fingers sought the electric switch. The next moment the room was full of light. He got out of bed, passed quickly through to his dressing-room, found the coat that he had worn that morning, and secured the booklet.

He went back again to bed, and, lying on his elbow, opened the dainty little printed thing and began to read thus:

"LONG ODDS"

"You don't say so! Where on earth has she gone?"

"I can't say, sir, but it's plain enough she *is* missing. Hasn't been seen since last night when she went up to her room."

I *was* put out, I own; my man on waking me had informed me that the cook was missing; she had gone to bed without anything being noticed amiss, and was now nowhere to be found. She was always an odd woman, but a capital cook. What had become of her? The very last sort of person to disappear in this way— a respectable elderly Scotchwoman—really quite a treasure in the country; and the more I thought of it while I dressed, the more puzzled I became. I hardly liked to send for the police; and then again it was awkward, very—people coming to dinner that day. It was really too bad.

But I had scarcely finished dressing when in rushed my man again. I do so dislike people being excited, and he was more than excited.

"Please, sir, Mr. Vend has come round to see you; his coachman has gone—went off in the night, and hasn't left a trace behind, and they say the gardener's boy is with him."

"Well," said I, "it is extraordinary; tell Mr. Vend I'm coming; stay, I'll go at once."

It was really past belief—the three of them! After an hour's talk with Vend, no explanation offered itself, so we decided to go to town as usual.

We walked down to the station, and saw at once something was wrong. Old Weeks, the stationmaster, was quite upset: his pointsman was missing, and the one porter had to take up his duty. However, the train coming up, we had no time to question him, but jumped in. There were three other people in the compartment, and really I thought I was going off my head when I heard what they were discussing. Vend, too, didn't seem to know if he was on his head or his heels. It was this that startled us so: "What can have become of them all?"

I heard no more. I really believe I swooned, but at the next station—a large one—we saw consternation on every face. I pinched myself to see if I was dreaming. I tried to persuade myself I was. Vend looked ghastly. A passenger got in; he did not look quite so dazed as some did, but savage and cross. For a time none spoke; at last someone said aloud—I don't think he expected an answer—

"What on earth's become of them?" and the cross looking man, who got in last, growled out,

"That's the worst of it; they are not *on earth,* they are gone. My boy always said it would be so; from the very first moment I heard it, I knew what had happened; often he has warned me. I still have his voice ringing in my ears.

"'I tell you, in *that night* there shall be two men in one bed: the one shall be taken, and the other shall be left.' (Luke xvii. 34.)

"I know only too well '*that night*' was *last* night. I've often prayed for it without thinking, and so I daresay have you: 'Thy kingdom come.' It makes me so savage I don't know what to do."

Now, I was an atheist, and did not believe the Bible. For the last thirty years (I am past fifty) I had stuck to my opinions, and when I heard men talk religious trash I invariably objected.

But this seemed altogether different. I tell you, for a thousand pounds I couldn't have said a word. I just hoped it would all turn out a dream, but the further we went, the more certain it became that we were all awake, and that by some unaccountable visitation of Providence a number of people had suddenly disappeared in the night.

The whole of society was unhinged; everybody had to do somebody's else's work. For instance, at the terminus, a porter had been put into Smith's stall, as the usual man was missing. Cabs were not scarce, but some of those who drove them seemed unlicensed and new to their work. The shutters in some of the shops were up, and on getting to my bank I heard the keys had only just been found.

Everyone was silent, and afraid lest some great misfortune was coming. I noticed we all seemed to mistrust one another, and yet as each fresh clerk, turned up late, entered the counting-room, a low whisper went round. The chief cashier, as I expected, did not come. The newspapers no one cared to look at; there seemed a tacit opinion that *they* could tell us nothing.

Business was at a standstill. I saw that very soon. I hoped as the day wore on that it would revive, but it did not. The clerks went off without asking my permission, and I was left alone. I felt I hated them. I did not know what to do. I could not well leave, else they might say the bank had stopped payment, and yet I felt I could not stay there. Business seemed to have lost its interest, and money its value. I put up the shutters myself, and at once noticed what a change had come over the City while I had been at the bank. *Then* all were trying to fill the void places; *now* it seemed as if the attempt had failed.

In the City some of the streets had that dismal Sunday appearance, while a few houses had been broken into; but in the main thoroughfares there was a dense mass of people, hurrying, it struck me, they knew not where. Some seemed dazed, others almost mad with terror. At the stations confusion reigned, and I heard there had been some terrible accidents. I went into my club, but the waiters had gone off without leave, and one had to help oneself.

As evening came on, I saw the lurid reflection of several fires, but, horrible to say, no one seemed to mind, and I felt myself that if the whole of London were burnt, and I with it, I should not care. For the first time in my life I no longer feared Death: I rather looked on him as a friend.

As the gas was not lit, and darkness came down upon us, one heard cries and groans. I tried to light the gas, but it was not turned on. I remembered there was a taper in the writing-room. I went and lit it, but of course it did not last long. I groped my way into the dining-room, and helped myself to some wine, but I could not find much, and what I took seemed to have no effect; and when I heard voices, they fell on me as if I were in a dream. They were talking of the Bible, though, and it now seemed the one book worth thinking of, yet in our vast club library I doubt if I should have found a single copy.

One said: "What haunts me are the words 'Watch therefore.' You can't *watch* *n*ow."

I thought of my dinner party. Little had I imagined a week ago, when I issued the invitations, how I should be passing the hour.

Suddenly I remembered the secretary had been a religious fanatic, and I made my way slowly to his room, knocking over a table, in my passage, with glasses on it. It fell with a crash which sounded through the house, but no one noticed it. By the aid of a match I saw candles on his writing table and lit them. Yes! as I thought, there was his Bible. It was open as if he had been reading it when called away, and another book I had never seen before lay alongside of it—a sort of index.

The Bible was open at Proverbs, and these verses, being marked, caught my eye:

"Because I have called and ye refused, I have stretched out My hand and no man regarded; I also will laugh at your calamity; I will mock when your fear cometh."

I had never thought before of God laughing—of God mocking. I had fancied man alone did that. Man's laughing had ended now—I saw that pretty plain.

I had a hazy recollection of a verse that spoke of men wanting the rocks to fall on them; so looked it up in the index. Yes, there was the word "Rock," and some of the passages were marked with a pencil. One was Deut. xxxii. 15: "He forsook God which made him, and lightly esteemed the Rock of our Salvation."

Perhaps he marked that passage after he had had a talk with me. How well I remember the earnestness with which he pressed salvation upon me that day—explaining the simplicity of trusting Christ and His blood for pardon—and assuring me that if I only yielded myself to the Lord I should understand the peace and joy he talked about. But it was no use. I remember I only chaffed him, and said mockingly that his God was a myth, and time would prove it, and he answered,

"Never. 'Heaven and earth shall pass away, but My Word shall not pass away.' He may come to-night."

I laughed and said, "What odds will you take? I lay you long ones."

Another passage marked was I. Samuel ii. 2, "Neither is there any rock like our God," and lower still "Man who built his house upon a rock."

I had no need to look that out. I knew what it referred to, and then my eye caught Matt. xxvii. 51, "The earth did quake, and the rocks rent." That was when Christ died to save sinners, died to save me—and yet I had striven against Him all my life. I could not bear to read more. I shut the book and got up. There were some texts hanging over the fireplace:

"Repent ye therefore, and be converted, that your sins may be blotted out."—Acts iii. 19.

"The blood of Jesus Christ His son cleanseth us from all sin."—I John i. 7.

"Now is the accepted time; behold, now is the day of salvation."—2 Cor. vi. 2.

As I turned to leave the room these caught my eye, and I said, "Well, I have been a fool."

Tom Hammond looked up from the little booklet,—a look of bewilderment was in his eyes, a sense of blankness, almost of stupefaction, in his mind. Like one who, half stunned, passes through some strange and wondrous experience, and slowly recalls every item of that experience as fuller consciousness returns, he went, mentally, slowly over the story of the little book.

"The verisimilitude of the whole story is little less than startling," he murmured. His eyes dropped upon the book again, and he read the last line aloud: "Well, I have been a fool."

Slowly, meditatively, he added: "And I, with every other otherwise sane man who has been careless as to whether such things are to be, am as big a fool as the man in that book!"

He laid the dainty little messenger down on the table by his bedside. His handling of the book was almost reverential. Reaching to the electric lever, he switched off the light. He wanted to think, and he could think best in the dark.

"Of course, I know *historically,*" he mused, "all the events of the Christ's life, His death, His resurrection, and—and—— Well, *there,* I think, my knowledge ends. In a vague way I have always known that the Bible said something of a great final denouement to all the World Drama—an award time of some kind, a millennium of perfect—perfect—well perfect everything that is peaceful and——Oh, I don't know much about it, after all. I am very much in a fog. I see, for Mrs. Joyce and that booklet both speak of a return of Christ into the air, whither certain dead and certain living are to be caught up to be with Him and to begin an eternity of bliss."

For a moment or two he tried to disentangle his many thoughts; then, with a weary little sigh, he gave up the task, murmuring: "*I* certainly am not ready for any such event. If there is to be a hideous leaving behind of the *un*ready, then I should be left to all that unknown hideousness."

A myriad thoughts crowded upon his brain. He gave up, at length, the perplexing attempt to think out the problem, telling himself that with the coming of the new day he would begin a definite search for the real facts of this great mystery—the second coming of Christ.

By an exercise of his will he finally settled himself to sleep.

CHAPTER XII.

THE CENTRE OF THE EARTH.

WILL you come into my workroom, Mr. Hammond? It is a kind of sanctum to me as well as a workroom, and I always feel that I can talk freer there than anywhere else."

It was the Jew, Abraham Cohen, who said these words. His visitor was Tom Hammond. It was the morning after that Tom Hammond had been troubled about "Long Odds" and its mysterious subject.

Jew and Gentile had had a few moments' general talk in the sitting-room downstairs, but Cohen wanted to see his visitor alone—to be where nothing should interrupt their conversation.

Tom Hammond's first vision of Cohen's workroom amazed him. As we have seen before, the apartment was a large one, and, besides being a workroom, partook of the character of a study, den, sanctum—anything of that order that best pleases the reader.

But it was the finished work which chiefly arrested the attention of Tom Hammond, and in wondering tones he cried: "It is all so exquisitely wrought and fashioned! But *what* can it be for?"

Cohen searched his visitor's face with his deep grave eyes.

"Will you give me your word, Mr. Hammond," he asked, "that you will hold in strictest confidence the fact that this work is here in this place, if I tell you what it is for?"

"I do give you my word of honour, Mr. Cohen." As

he spoke, Tom Hammond held forth his hand. The Jew
grasped the hand, there was an exchange of grips; then
as their clasp parted, the Jew said:

"I do not wish to bind you to any secrecy as to the
fact that such work as this is being performed in England, but only that you should preserve the secret of
the whereabouts of the work and workers." With a
sudden glow of pride—it flashed in his eyes, it rang in
his tones—he cried, "This work is for the New Temple!"

"The New Temple? I don't think I quite understand
you, Mr. Cohen. Where is this temple being built?"
There was amaze in Tom Hammond's voice.

"It is not yet begun," replied the Jew. "That is, the
actual rearing has not yet begun, though the preparations are well forward. The New Temple is to be at
Jerusalem, Mr. Hammond."

The ring of pride deepened in his voice as he went
on: "There can be no other site for the Temple of
Jehovah save Zion, the city of our God, beautiful for
situation, the joy of the whole earth—the centre of the
world, Mr. Hammond."

As he talked, Tom Hammond, watching him intently
saw how the soul of the man and the hope of the true
Israelite shone out of his eyes.

Crossing the room to where a chart of the world
(on Mercator's Projection) hung on the wall, the Jew
took an inch-marked straight-edge, and laying one end
of it on Barrow Point, Alaska, he marked the spot on the
straight-edge where it touched Jerusalem. From Jerusalem to Wrangel Land, Siberia, farthest east, he showed
by his straight-edge that practically he got the same
measurement as when from the west. From Jerusalem
to North Cape, Scandinavia, and from Jerusalem to the

Cape of Good Hope, he showed again was each practically the same distance.

"Always, always, is Zion the centre of the inhabited earth!' he cried in quiet, excited tones. Moving quickly back to Hammond's side, he said: "Did you ever think of this, sir, that, practically speaking, all the nations west of Jerusalem (those of Europe) write from west to east—that is, towards the city of our God; whilst all the Asiatic races (those east of Zion) write from east to west—just the opposite,—but always *towards* Zion? No, no, sir; there can be no other place on earth for the New Temple of Jehovah save Jerusalem. Read Ezekiel, from the fortieth chapter, sir, and you will see how glorious a Temple Jehovah is to have soon. 'Show the house to the people of Israel,' God said in vision to His prophet, 'and let them build it after the sum, the pattern which I show you.' And that, sir, is what we are doing."

"Who are the *we* who are doing this?" Tom Hammond's face was as full of wonder as his voice. "Who," he continued, "makes the plans, gives the orders, finds the funds?"

"Wealthy, patriotic men of our people, sir. We as a race are learning that soon the Messiah will come, and we are proving our belief by preparing for the House of our God. Italian Jews all over Italy are carving the richest marbles; wrought iron, wondrous works in metal, gold and silver ornaments, cornices, chapiters, bells for the high priest's robes, and a myriad other things are being prepared; so that the moment the last restriction on our land—the land of our fathers, the land which Jehovah gave unto our forefather Abraham, saying, 'Your seed shall possess it'—is removed, we shall begin to snip the several prepared parts of the Temple to Palestine, as the Gentiles term our land."

A curious little smile flittered over his face as he added.

"The very march of modern times in the East, Mr. Hammond, is all helping to make the consummation of our work more easy. The new railways laid from the coast to Jerusalem are surely part of the providence of our God. When Messiah comes, sir, we shall be waiting ready for Him, I trust."

"But do you not know," Tom Hammond interrupted, "that according to every record of history as well as the New Testament, all Christendom has believed, for all the ages since, that the Messiah came nearly two thousand years ago?"

"The *Nazarene?*"

There was as much or more of pity than scorn in the voice of the Jew as he uttered the word.

"How could *He* be the Messiah, sir? he went on. "Could any good thing come out of Nazareth? Besides, *our Messiah* is to redeem Israel, to deliver them from the hand of the oppressor, and to gather again into one nation all our scattered race. No, no! a thousand times No! The Nazarene could not be *our* Messiah?"

Turning quickly to Hammond, he asked, "Are *you* a Christian, sir?"

For a moment Tom Hammond was startled by the suddenness, the definiteness, of the question. He found no immediate word of reply.

"You are a *Gentile,* of course, Mr. Hammond," the Jew went on; "but are you a Christian? For it is a curious fact that I find very few Gentiles whom I have met, even *professed* Christians, and fewer still who ever pretend to live up to their profession."

Tom Hammond recovered himself sufficiently to say:

"Yes, I am a Gentile, of course, and I *suppose* I am —er——"

It struck him, as he floundered in the second half of his reply, as being very extraordinary that he should find it difficult to state why he supposed he was a Christian. While he hesitated the Jew went on:

"Why should you say you *suppose*, sir? Is there nothing distinctive enough about the possession of Christianity to give assurance of it to its possessor? I do not *suppose* I am a *Jew,* sir (by religion I mean, and not merely by race.) No, sir, I do not suppose, for I *know* it. There is all the difference in the world, it seems to me, sir, between the mere theology and the religion of the faith we profess. The religion is life, it seems to me, sir; theology is only the science of that life."

Both men were so utterly absorbed in their talk that they did not hear a touch on the handle of the door. It was only as it opened that they turned round. Zillah stood framed in the doorway. Cohen, who saw her every day, realized that she had never looked so radiantly beautiful before. She had almost burst into the room, but paused as she saw that a stranger was present.

"Excuse me," she began; "I had no idea you had a friend with you, Abraham."

She would have retreated, but he stopped her with an eager—

"Come in, Zillah."

She advanced, gazing in curious inquiry at Hammond.

"This is Mr. Tom Hammond, editor of the 'Courier,'

Zillah," Cohen explained to the young girl. To Hammond he added, "My wife's sister, Zillah Robart."

The introduced pair shook hands. The young Jew went on to explain to Zillah how the great editor came to be visiting him.

Tom Hammond's eyes were fixed upon the vision of loveliness that the Jewess made. She was going to assist at the wedding of a girl-friend, and had come to show herself to her brother-in-law before starting. Lovely at the most ordinary times, she looked perfectly radiant in her well-chosen wedding finery.

Tom Hammond had seen female loveliness in many lands—East, North, West, South. He had gazed upon women who seemed too lovely for earth—women whose flesh was alabaster, whose glance would woo emperors; women whose skins glowed with the olive of southern lands, the glance of whose black, lustrous eyes intoxicated the beholder in the first instant: Inez of Spain, Mousmec of Japan, Katrina of Russia, Carlotta of Naples, Rosie of Paris, Maggie of the Scottish Highlands, Patty of Wales, Kate of Ireland, and a score of other typical beauties. But this Jewish maiden, this Zillah of Finsbury—she was beyond all his thought or knowledge of feminine loveliness.

While Cohen talked on for a moment or two, and Zillah's eyes were fixed upon her brother-in-law, Tom Hammond's gaze was riveted upon the lovely girl.

Every feature of her beautiful face became photographed on his brain. Had he been a clever artist, he could have gone to his studio and have flung with burning, brilliant haste her face upon his canvas.

He thought of Zenobia as he looked upon her brow. He wondered if ever two such wide, black, lustrous eyes had ever shone in the face of a woman before, or whether a female soul had ever before been mirrored in such eyes.

Her mouth was not the large, wide feature so often seen in women of her race, but of exquisite lines, with ripe, full lips, as brilliant in colour as the most glowing coral. Her eyes were fringed with the blackest, finest, silkiest lashes. Her hair was raven in hue and wondrous in its wealth.

He realized, in that first moment of full gazing upon her, how faded every other female face must ever seem beside her glorious beauty. With a strange freak of mental conjuring, Madge Finisterre and that interrupted tete-a-tete rose up before him, and a sudden sense of relief swept over him that George Carlyon had returned at the moment that he did.

"It is all so strange, so wonderful to me, what I have seen and heard here," he jerked out as Cohen finished his explanation.

Hammond spoke to the beautiful girl, whose great lustrous eyes had suddenly come back to his face.

For a moment or two longer he voiced his admiration of the separate pieces of finished work, and spoke of his own growing interest in the Jewish race.

The great black eyes that gazed upwards into his, grew liquid with the evident emotion that filled the soul of the beautiful girl. With the frank, hearty, simple gesture of the perfectly unconventional woman, she held forth her hand to Hammond as she said:

"It is so good of you, sir, to speak thus of my brother-in-law's work and of our race. There are few who speak kindly of us. Even though, as a nation, you English give our poor persecuted people sanctuary, yet there are few who care for us or speak kindly of us, and fewer still who speak kindly to us."

Tom Hammond held the pretty, plump little hand that she offered him clasped warmly in his, almost forgetting himself as he gazed down into her expressive face and listened to her rich musical voice. There was an ardency in his gaze that was unknown, unrealized, by himself.

The olive of the girl's cheeks warmed under the power of his gaze. He, saw the warm colour rise, and remembered himself, shifted his eyes, and released her hand.

"I must not stay another moment, Abraham," she cried, turning to the Jew. "Adah would be vexed if I were late."

She turned back to Hammond, but before she could speak he was saying,

"Good-bye, Miss Robart; I hope we may meet again. What your brother has already told me only incites me to come again and see him, for there are many things I want to know."

He shook hands with the girl again. His eyes met hers, and again he saw the olive cheeks suddenly warm.

Ten minutes later he was driving back to his office, his mind in a strange whirl, the beautiful face of Zillah Robart filling all his vision.

He pulled himself up at last, and laughed low and amusedly as he murmured,

"And I am the man whose pulses had never been quickened by the sight or the touch of a woman until I met her——"

The memory of Madge Finisterre flashed into his mind. He smiled to himself as he mused:

"Even when I seemed most smitten by Madge, by her piquant Americanism, I told myself I was not sure that

love had anything to do with my feelings.   Now I
know it had not."

His eyes filled suddenly with a kind of staring wonder
as he cried out, in a low, startled undertone:

"Am I inferring to myself that this sudden admiration
for Zillah Robart has any element of love in it?"

He smiled at his own unuttered answer.   The cab
pulled up at the door of the office at that moment.   He
came back sharply to everyday things.

CHAPTER XIII

A DEMON.

MADGE FINISTERRE awoke early on the morning after that discussion with herself anent Hammond's possible proposal.

With startling suddenness, as she lay still a moment, a vision of the pastor of Balhang came up before her mind. Then a strang thing happened to her, for a yearning sense of home-sickness suddenly filled her.

She tried to laugh at herself for her "childishness, as she called it, and sprang from her bed to prepare for her bath. Standing for one instant by the bedside, she murmured:

"But, after all, it is time I was paddling across again. Who ever heard of anyone from our side staying here through the winter? I must think this all out seriously. Anyway, I'll get my bath, and dress, and go for a stroll before breakfast. They say that one ought to see suburban London pouring over the bridges into London city in the early morning. I'll go this morning."

Half-an-hour later she was dressed ready for her expedition. As she passed the office on her way out, they were sorting the morning mail. She waited for her letters. There was only one, but it was from home.

Racing back to her room, she tore it open with an eagerness born, unconsciously to herself, of the nostalgia that had seized upon her three-quarters of an hour before.

There were two large, closely-written sheets in the letter—one from her father and one from her mother. Each told their own news.

She read her father's first; every item interested her, though as she read she seemed to feel that there was all through it an underlying strain of longing for her return.

"Dear old poppa!" she murmured as she neared the finish of the epistle.

Suddenly her eyes took in the two lines of postscript jammed close into the bottom edge of the first sheet. Her heart seemed to stand still as she read:—

"Pastor is considered sick. Doctor can't make his case out."

"Pastor sick!" She gasped the words aloud; then, turning swiftly to her mother's letter, she cried: "Momma will tell more than this!"

Her eyes raced over the written lines. Her mother said a little more than her father had done about the sickness of their friend and pastor; not much, though, in actual words, but to the disturbed heart of the young girl there seemed to her much deeper meaning.

An excited trembling came upon her for a few moments. The next instant she had put a strong curb upon herself, and, folding the letters, and replacing them in the envelope, she cried out quietly, but sharply:

"The boat from Southampton sails at two to-day. I'll catch that!"

The next instant she was divesting herself of her hat and jacket, and began to set about her packing.

Now and again she talked to herself thus: "Sick, is he? Poor old pastor! I guess I know what's the matter with him, and I'll put him right in five minutes."

She smiled as she went on: "I guess, too, I've found out what's the matter with me—I want to be a pastor's wife!"

The next instant her voice was carolling out:

"For I tell them they need not come wooing of me,
  For my heart, my heart, is over the sea."

Her fingers were busy, her mind all the time kept mentally arranging a host of things.

"I wonder," she murmured presently, "how Uncle Archibald and George will take my sudden departure? Well, I'm glad George is out of town. He's been showing signs of spoons lately with me, so it's best, perhaps, that I should get off without seeing him."

*   *   *   *   *   *   *

By eleven that forenoon she had left Waterloo. Her uncle had seen her off from the station. He wanted to accompany her to Southampton, but she would not hear of it.

"I want to be very quiet all the way down," she said, "and write some important letters. Make my excuses to everybody, and explain that I only had an hour or two to do everything."

At the last moment her uncle slipped an envelope into her hand, saying, "You are not to open it until you have been travelling a quarter of an hour."

Then came the good-byes, and—off.

She had been travelling *nearly* a quarter of an hour when she opened the envelope. There was a brief, hearty, loving note inside, in her uncle's hand-writing, expressing the joy her visit had given him, and his sense of loneliness at her going, and saying:

"Please, dear Madge, accept the enclosure in second envelope, as a souvenir of your visit, from your affectionate

"Nunkums."

She opened the smaller envelope. To her breathless amazement, she found a Bank of England note for £1,000. When she recovered herself a little, a smile filled her eyes as she murmured:

"Fancy an American Methodist pastor's wife with a thousand pounds of her own! My!"

The train was rushing on; she remembered that she had a special letter to write. She opened her bag and took out writing materials. The carriage rocked tremendously, but she managed to pen her letter. Before she finally enclosed the letter in an envelope, she took from her purse a two-inch cutting from the columns of some newspaper or magazine. This she placed in the letter.

*   *   *   *   *   *   *

Tom Hammond had just settled himself down to work when a letter, bearing the Southampton post-mark, was delivered to him. Opening it, and reading "My dear Mr. Hammond," he turned next to the signature. "Madge Finisterre?" he cried softly, surprisedly, under his breath. Wonderingly he turned back to the first page, and read:

"You will be surprised to know that when you receive this I shall be steaming down Channel *en route* for New York. I got letters from home this morning that made it imperative that I should start at once.

"I cannot leave without thanking you for all your kindness to me. It has been a pleasure to have known you, and I sincerely hope that we may meet again some day.

"Now I am going to take you right into my confidence, Mr. Hammond, for who so discreet as a 'prophet?'—vide 'The Courier.'

"Yesterday evening, after dinner, I had a long talk alone with myself. I had had a very pleasant tete-a-tete tea with a friend—perhaps you may remember this,—and while I went over in mind many things in connection with that tete-a-tete, especially the events immediately preceding the interruption, I suddenly realized a sense of longing for home.

"A night or two before I sailed from America, our pastor asked me to be his wife. He was awfully in earnest, poor fellow; and I could see how love for me—gay, frivolous little me—was consuming him. I was startled at the proposition, and told him frankly that I did not know my own mind, but that if ever I found out that I loved him, I would come right away and tell him so. I found out this morning, when I heard that he was dangerously sick, that I wanted him as much as ever he wanted me. At this stage of the letter, please read the cutting enclosed."

Wondering what the clipping could have to do with the subject, Tom Hammond laid down the letter and read the cutting:

"A king had a son born to him in his old age, and was warned by his astrologers and physicians, that his son would be blind if he ever saw the light before he was twelve years old. Accordingly the king built for him a subterranean chamber, where he was kept till he was past the fatal age. Thereupon he was taken out from his retreat, and shown all the beauties of the world, gold and jewels and arms, and carriages and horses, and beautiful dresses. But seeing some women pass, he asked what they might be, and was told, 'Demons, who lead men astray.' Afterwards the king asked him which of all the beautiful things he had seen he desired most, and the prince answered, "The demons which lead men astray."

"I am going back to be demon to my pastor," the letter went on, "to lead him—not astray, I trust, but back to health. Please keep all this in absolute confidence, for I have not given even a hint of it to my uncle. Whenever you visit the States, be sure to come and visit me, for no one will be more welcome from the Old Country than yourself.

"By-the-bye, dear friend, apropos of your remark anent the presence of a woman to make tea for you, keep the subject well before yourself, and when you see the lady who can really satisfy all your ideals, propose quickly, secure her, and—happy thought—do America by way of a honeymoon, and come and see me.

"Yours most sincerely,

"MADGE FINISTERRE."

He smiled as he laid down the letter. For a moment all the bright, piquant personality of the writer filled his vision. Then, with a swiftness and completeness that was almost startling, her face vanished from his mental picturing, and Zillah Robart, in all her radiant loveliness, took the place in his thought and vision.

For a brief while he was absorbed in his new vision. The sudden entrance of Ralph Bastin dispelled his dreaming.

After a few moments' talk, Bastin cried, quite excit-

edly, "I say, Tom, those pars of yours about the Jews
are the talk of all London—our London, I mean, of
course."

Without breaking the confidence reposed in him by
Cohen, Tom Hammond told his friend what he had
recently discovered as to the Jewish work on the materials for the New Temple.

"That's strange, Tom," returned Bastin. "I dropped
in now as much as anything to tell you that last night
I met Dolly Anstruther—you remember her, don't you?
—the little Yorkshire girl that was learning sculpture
when we were staying at Paris with Montmarte.

"She has just come back from Italy, where she has
been three years. She told me how startled she was
to hear from several sources about this New Temple
business. She said she visited a very large studio in
Milan, and saw the most magnificent pillar she had
ever seen. She asked the great artist what it was for,
and he said, 'It is a pillar for the New Temple at
Jerusalem.'

"In Rome she visited another great studio, and there
she saw a duplicate of the Milan pillar, and was told
again, 'Oh, that is a pillar for the future Temple at
Jerusalem.'

"In another place, where the most wonderful brass-
work in the world is turned out, she saw two magnificent gates; and, on inquiring where they were des-
tined to be hung, received the same reply, 'In the future
Temple at Jerusalem.' What does it all mean, Tom?"
he added.

"That is what I want to find out, to be perfectly
sure of, Ralph. My intelligent Jew, of whom I told
you, declares that the Messiah is coming. We, as Chris-

tians—nominal Christians, I mean, of course,—same as you and I, Ralph, don't profess anything more——"

Bastin searched his friend's face with a sudden keenness, but did not interrupt him by asking him what he meant.

"As nominal Christians," Tom Hammond went on, "we believe the Christ has already come. But the question has been aroused in my mind of late (suggested by certain things that I have not time to go into now), does the Bible teach that Christ is coming again, and are all these strange movings among the Jews and in the politics of the world so many signs and——"

There came an interruption at that moment. The tape was telling of the assassination of a Continental crowned head. Both men became journalists, pure and simple, in an instant.

CHAPTER XIV.

MAJOR H—— ON "THE COMING!"

TOM HAMMOND was riding westwards in the Tube. It was the morning after the events narrated in the last chapter. He had just bought from a book-stall a volume of extracts from essays on art in all its branches. He sat back in the comfortable seat of the car dipping into the book. Suddenly an extract arrested his attention.

It was evidently a description of the Crucifixion, but —most tantalizing—the head of this page was torn, he could find out nothing about the authorship. But the extract interested him:—

"Darkness—sooty, portentous darkness—shrouds the whole scene; only above the accursed wood, as if through a horrid rift in the murky ceiling, a rainy deluge—'sleety-flaw, discoloured water'—streams down amain, spreading a grisly, spectral light, even more horrible than that palpable night. Already the Earth pants thick and fast! The darkened Cross trembles! The winds are dropt—the air is stagnant—a muttering rumble growls underneath their feet, and some of the miserable crowd begin to fly down the hill. The horses sniff the coming terror, and become unmanageable through fear. The moment rapidly approaches, when, nearly torn asunder by His own weight, fainting with loss of blood, which now runs in narrower rivulets from His slit veins, His temples and breast drowned in sweat, and His black tongue parched with the fiery death-fever, Jesus cried, 'I thirst.' The deadly vinegar is elevated to Him.

"His head sinks, and the sacred corpse 'swings senseless on the cross.' A sheet of vermilion flame shoots sheer through the air and vanishes; the rocks of Carmel and Lebanon cleave asunder; the sea rolls on high from the sands its black, weltering waves. Earth yawns, and the graves give up their dwellers. The dead and the living are mingled together in unnatural conjunction, and hurry through the Holy City.

"New prodigies await them there. The veil of the Temple—the unpierceable veil—is rent asunder from top to bottom, and that dreaded recess, containing the Hebrew mysteries—the fatal ark, with the tables and seven-branched candelabrum—is disclosed by the light of unearthly flames to the God-deserted multitude."

"Strange!" he mused, as his eyes stared into space, his mind occupied with the thought of the extract. "Strange how everything of late seems to be compelling my attention to the Christ—Christ past, Christ future."

At that instant he heard someone mention the name of his paper. He glanced in the direction of the voices. Two gentlemen were talking together. It was evident that his own identity was utterly unknown to them.

"You're right, you're right," the second man was saying. "A very clever fellow, evidently, that editor of the *Courier.*"

"You have noticed, of course," the first man went on, "those striking paragraphs, of late, about the Jews. Though, to a keen student of the subject, they show a very superficial knowledge; still, it is refreshing to find a modern newspape · editor writing like that at all."

"Yes," the other said, "but it is strange how few

people, even Christian people, ever realize how intimately the future of the Jewish race is bound up with that other shamefully neglected truth—the coming of the Lord for His Church. I wish the editor of the *Courier,* and every other newspaper editor, could be induced to go this afternoon and hear Major H—— speak on these things at the —— Room."

"British Museum!" called the conductor of the car. The two talkers got out. Tom Hammond also alighted. As he mounted in the lift to the street, he decided that he would hear this major on the subject that was occupying his own perplexed thought so much.

Three o'clock that afternoon found him one of a congregation of three to four hundred persons in the —— Room. He was amazed at the quality of the audience. He recognized quite a dozen well-known London clergymen and ministers, with a score of other equally well-known laymen—literary men, merchants, etc. All were of a superior class. There was a large sprinkling of ladies, who, in many cases, were evidently sisters. Unaccustomed to such meetings, Tom Hammond did not know how enormous is the number of Christian women who are to be found at special religious gatherings, conventions, etc.

There was a subdued hum of whispering voices in the place. The hum suddenly ceased. Tom Hammond glanced quickly towards the platform. Half-a-dozen gentlemen and one or two ladies were taking their seats there. They bowed their heads in silent prayer.

A minute later a tall, fine looking man, the centre one of the platform group, rose to his feet and advanced to the rail. He held a hymn-book in his hand. His keen eyes swept the faces of the gathered people. Then ın a clear, ringing voice like the voice of a military officer on the battle-field, he cried:

"Number three-twenty-four. Let every voice ring out in song."

Tom Hammond opened the linen-covered book that had been handed to him as he entered, and was almost startled to note the likeness of the sentiment of the hymn to the poem of B. M., which had struck him so forcibly that night in his office.

The major gave out the first verse:

> "It may be at morn, when the day is awaking,
>   When sunlight thro' darkness and shadow is breaking,
>   That Jesus will come in the fulness of glory,
>   To take out of the world 'His own.'"

The major paused a moment to interpolate, "Let the gladness of the thought ring out in your voices as you sing, but especially in the chorus."

> "O Lord Jesus, how long?
> How long ere we shout the glad song
>   Christ returneth! Hallelujah!
>   Hallelujah! Amen!"

The singing of that hymn was a revelation to Tom Hammond. He had heard hearty, ringing, triumphant song at Handel festivals, etc., but among the rank and file, so to speak, of Christians he had never heard anything like the singing of that verse and chorus.

A hundred thoughts and conflicting emotions filled him as he realized, as the hymn went on, that these people were really inspired by the glorious hope of the return of the Christ. Once he shuddered as the thought presented itself to his mind,

"How should *I* fare if this Christ came suddenly—came now?"

Twice over the last verse was sung, the quiet rapture of the singers being doubly accentuated as the glorious words rang out:

> "Oh, joy! oh, delight! should we go without dying!
> No sickness, no sadness, no dread, and no crying;
> Caught up through the clouds with our Lord into glory,
>   When Jesus receives 'His own.'"

With the last-sung note the voice of the Major rang out again:

"General Sir R. P.—— will lead us in prayer."

The hush that followed was of the tensest. It lasted a full half-minute, then the old general's voice led in a prayer such as Tom Hammond had never even conceived possible to human lips, and such as, certainly, he had never heard before. It awed him, and at the same time revealed to him that real Christianity was something which he, with all his knowledge of men and things, had never before come in contact with.

The prayer concluded, not a moment was wasted. In his clear, ringing tones, the major began:

"Turn with me, if you will, dear friends, to the first chapter of the Acts of the Apostles, and the eleventh verse."

Tom Hammond wished that he had a Bible with him. It seemed to him that he was the only person there without one. In an instant every Bible was opened at the passage named. There was no searching, no fumbling. This was another revelation to him.

"They know their Bibles," he mused, "better than I do my dictionary or encyclopædia."

But his attention was suddenly riveted on the major, who, pocket Bible in hand, was saying;

"Suffer me, friends, to change one word in my reading, that the truth may come home clearer to our hearts. 'Ye men of London, . . . This same Jesus which is taken up from you into heaven shall so come in like manner as ye have seen Him go into heaven.' "

He paused for one instant, then went on: "The second coming of our Lord and Saviour Jesus Christ is, I believe, the central truth of real, true Christianity at this moment, and it should be carefully, diligently studied by every converted soul. It should be comprehended as far as Scripture reveals it, and so apprehended that we should live in daily, hourly expectancy of that return. Moody, the great evangelist, to whom the whole subject (as he tells us) was once most objectionable, upon studying the Word of God for himself, in this connection, was so profoundly impressed with the insistence with which the return of the Lord was emphasized, that he was compelled to believe in it, and to preach it, saying, 'It is almost the most precious truth of all the Bible. Why, one verse in thirteen throughout the New Testament is said to allude to this wondrous subject in some form or another.'

"Many of you who are present this afternoon are not only conversant with this glorious matter, but are living in the glad expectancy of the return of your Lord. But there are sure to be some here to-day to whom the whole subject is foreign, and to you—even if there be only one such—I shall speak as plainly, frankly, simply, yearningly, as though we were tete-a-tete.

CHAPTER XV.

THE ADDRESS.

"NOW to begin. Even in the Church of God there are whole multitudes to whom the very title of this afternoon's address is but jargon. They will not search the Word for it, they will barely tolerate its mention. Why? 'Oh,' say some, 'hidden things are not to be searched into.' Others there are who spiritualize every reference to the Lord's second coming, and say, 'Yes, of course, He has come again, He has come into my heart, or how else could I have become a child of God.'

"To these last, these dreamers, we would respectfully say, 'A coming into the air for His people, to take them up, is a totally different thing to coming into the heart to indwell as Saviour and Keeper while we are travelling life's pathway.'

"There is another section of the Christian Church who say, 'We do not want to hear anything about it. Our minister don't hold with it; it is not a doctrine of our church.' Now, such an argument as this is blasphemous, since, if God has put it into His Word, it is blasphemy to ignore it, to refuse to believe it.

"Two distinct advents are plainly taught in Scripture. The first, of Jesus' birth as a Babe in Bethlehem, the second as 'Son of Man'—glorified, who shall come in the clouds. Now, every Christian will admit, nay, more, the very worldling admits the fact that every Scripture relating to the first advent, as to time, place, circumstances, was literally fulfilled, even to the minutest detail. Then, in the name of common-sense, with the same covenant Scriptures in our hands, why should we not expect to see the predictions relating to the second advent also fulfilled to the very letter?

"We have our Lord's own definite promise in John fourteen: 'If I go, I will come again and receive you unto Myself.' We are all agreed that He went. Well, in the same breath He said, 'I will come again.' Can any English be plainer—'And receive you unto Myself?' That promise cannot allude to conversion, and it certainly cannot allude to death, for death is a going to Him —if we are saved.

"This expectancy of Christ's return for His people was the only hope of the early Church; and over and over again, in a variety of ways in the epistles it is shown to be the only hope of the Church, until that Church is taken out of the world, as a bride is taken by the bridegroom from her old home, to dwell henceforth in his. There never has been any comfort to bereaved ones in the thought of death, nor to any one of us who are living is there any comfort in the contemplation of death, save and except, of course, the thought of relief from weariness and suffering, and in being translated to a painless sphere, to be with Christ. But in the contemplation of the coming of Christ, when the dead in Christ shall rise, and those who are in Christ, who are still living when He comes, there is the certainty of the gladdest meeting when all are 'caught up together in the air, to be for ever with the Lord.' No waiting until the end of the world but, if He came this afternoon— and this may happen—you who have loved ones with Christ would that very instant meet them in the air, with your Lord."

Tom Hammond listened intently to every word of the major's, and, as Scripture after Scripture was referred to, he saw how the speaker's statements were all verified by the Word of God.

"There are two points I would emphasize here," the major went on. "First, that we must not confuse the second coming of the Lord—the coming in the air—for His saints, with that later coming, probably seven years after, when He shall come with His saints to reign.

"And, secondly, to those to whom this whole subject may be new, I would say, you must not confuse the second coming of our Lord with the end of the world. The uninstructed, inexperienced child of God feels a quaking of heart at all talk of such a coming.

"Such people shrink from the suddenness of it. They say that there is no preparatory sign to warn us of that coming. But that is not true.

"The Word of God gives many instructions as to the signs of Christ's near return, and the hour we live in shows us these signs on every hand, so that it is only those who are ignorant of the Word of God, or those who are carelessly or wilfully blind to the signs around (and this applies, we grieve to say, as much to ministers as to people,) who fail to see how near must be the moment of our Lord's return.

"The first sign of this return is an awakening of national life among the Jews, that shall immediately precede their return—in unbelief—to their own land. Please turn with me to Matthew twenty-four."

There was again that soft rustle of turning leaves that had struck Tom Hammond as so remarkable. Someone behind him, at the same instant, passed a Bible, open at the reference, to him over his shoulder. With a grateful glance and a murmured word of thanks, he accepted the loan of the book.

"I will read a verse or two here and there," the major announced. "You who know your Bibles, friends, will readily recall the subject-matter of the previous chapter, and how our Lord after His terrible prediction upon Jerusalem, added, 'Behold, your house is left unto you desolate. For I say unto you, Ye shall not see Me henceforth, till ye shall say, Blessed is He that cometh in the name of the Lord.'

"This is Jewish, of course, but the whole matter of the future of the Jews and of the return of the Lord for His Church, and, later on, with His Church, are bound up together. Presently, after uttering His last prediction, the disciples came to Him privately, saying,

" 'Tell us, when shall these things be? and what shall be the sign of Thy coming, and of the end of the world?"

"Keep your Bibles open where you now have them, friends, and note this—that the two-fold answer of our Lord's is in the reverse order to the disciples' question. In verses four and five He points out what should not be the sign of His coming. While, in verse six, He shows what should not be the sign of the end of the world. With these distinctions I shall have more to say another day.

"This afternoon I want to keep close to the signs of the coming of the Lord. Read then the thirty-second and third verses: 'Now learn a parable of the fig-tree: when its branch is yet tender, and putteth forth leaves, ye know that summer is nigh: so likewise ye, when ye shall see all these things, know that'—look in the margins of your Bible, please, and note that the 'it' of the text becomes 'He,' which is certainly the only wise translation—'when ye shall see all these things, know that He is near, even at your doors.'

"Now, I hardly need remind the bulk of you, friends, gathered here this afternoon, that the figtree, in the Gospels, represents Israel. The Bible uses three trees to represent Israel at different periods of her history, and in different aspects of her responsibility.

"The Old Testament uses the vine as the symbol of Israel, the Gospels the fig, and the Epistles the olive. At your leisure, friends, if you have never studied this, do so. You will not be puzzled much over the blasting of the barren fig-tree when you have made a study of the whole of this subject, because you will see that it was parabolic of God's judgment on the unfruitful Jewish race.

"Now, with this key of interpretation before us, how pointed becomes this first sign of the return of our Lord. 'When,' He says, 'the fig-tree putteth forth her leaves' —when the Jewish nation shows signs of a revival of national life and vitality,—'then know that the coming of the Lord draweth nigh.'

"The careful reader of the daily press, even though not a Christian, ought to have long ago been awakened to the startling fact that, after thousands of years, the national life of Israel is awakening. The Jew is returning to his own land—Palestine.

"Only a year or two ago the world was electrified by hearing of the formation of that wonderful Zionist movement. How it has spread and grown! And how, ever since, the increasing thousands have been flocking back to Palestine! There are now nearly three times the number of Jews in and around Jerusalem, that there were after the return from the Babylonish captivity. Agricultural settlements are extending all over the land. Vineyards and olive-grounds are springing up everywhere.

"Now note a remarkable fulfilment of prophecy. Turn to Isaiah xvii. 10, 11: 'Therefore shalt thou plant pleasant plants, and shalt set it with strange slips. In the day thou shalt make thy plant to grow, and in the morning shalt thou make thy seed to flourish; but the harvest shall be a heap in the day of grief and of desperate sorrow.'

"In the early months of eighteen-ninety-four the Jews ordered two million vine-slips from America, which they planted in Palestine. There is the fulfillment of the first part of that prophecy, and if we are justified in believing, as we think we are, that the return of the Lord is imminent, then, as the tribulation will doubtless immediately follow that return, and of the taking out of the Church from the world, then the great gathering in of the harvest of those vines will be in 'the day of grief and of desperate sorrow.'

"Now, let me read to you, friends, an extract from the testimony of an expert, long resident in Palestine:

"'There is not the shadow of a doubt,' he writes, 'as to the entire changing of the climate of the land here (Palestine.) The former and latter rains are becoming the regular order of the seasons, and this is doubtless due (physically, I mean) to the fact that the new colonists are planting trees everywhere where they settle. The land, for thousands of years, has been denuded of trees, so that there was nothing to attract the clouds, etc.

"'Comparing the rainfall for the last five years, I find that there has been about as much rain in April as in March; whereas, comparing five earlier years, from 1880-85, I find that the rainfall in April was considerably less than in March, and if we go back farther still, we find that rain in April was almost unknown.

"'Thus God is preparing the land for the people. The people, too, are being prepared for the land. The day is fast approaching when 'the Lord will arise and have mercy upon Zion.'

"I need hardly, I think, tell you what even the secular press has been giving some most striking articles about quite recently,—namely, the quiet preparation on the part of the Jews of everything for the rebuilding of the temple at Jerusalem.

"I see, by the lighting up of your faces, that you are familiar with the fact that gates, pillars, marbles, ornaments, and all else requisite for the immediate building of the new temple are practically complete, and only await the evacuation of the hideous Mohamedan, with all his abominations, from Jerusalem, to be hurried to the site of the old temple, and to be reared, a new temple to Jehovah, by the Jew. Any day, Turkey—'the sick man of the East'—in desperate straits for money, may sell Palestine to the Jews.

"The Jews are to return to their land in unbelief of Christ being the Messiah. They will build their temple, reorganize the old elaborate services, the lamb will be slain again 'between the two evenings,' and—but all else of this time belongs to another address. What we have to see this afternoon is that the fig-tree—the Jewish nation—is budding, and to hear Jesus Christ saying to us, 'When ye see all these things, know that He is near, even at the doors.'

"Another sign of the return of our Lord is to be the

world-wide preaching of the Gospel. Now, in this connection, let me give a word of correction of a common error on this point.

"The Bible nowhere gives a hint that the world is to be converted before the return of the Lord for His Church. As a matter of fact, the world—the times—are to grow worse and worse; more polished, more cultured, cleverer, better educated, yet grosser in soul, falser in worship. The bulk of the Church shall have the form of godliness, but deny the power.

"Men shall be 'lovers of their own selves'—who can deny that selfishness is not a crowning sin of this age? —'covetous'—look at the heaping up of riches, at the cost of the peace, the honour, the very blood of others, —'incontinent'—the increase in our divorce court cases is alarming, disgusting,—'lovers of pleasure'—the whole nation has run mad on pleasures.

"I need not enlarge further on this side of the subject, save to repeat that the Word of God is most plain and emphatic on this point, that the return of our Lord is to be marked by a fearful declension from vital godliness. But, with all this, there is to be a world-wide proclamation of the truth of salvation in Jesus. Not necessarily that every individual soul shall hear it, but that all nations, etc., shall have it preached to them.

"Now, in this connection, let me mention a fact that has deeply impressed me. It is this, that the greatest reawakening in the hearts of individual Christians in all the churches—England, America, the Colonies—as testified to by all concerned, agrees, in time, with the awakening of the Church of Christ to the special need of intercession for foreign missions—namely, from 1873-75.

"I must close for this afternoon, lest I weary you.

We will, God willing, come together again here on Tuesday at the same hour, and I pray you all to be much in prayer for blessing on the attempt to open up these wondrous truths, and pray also that the right kind of people may be gathered in. ˙ Will you all work for this, as well as pray for it? Invite people to the meetings.

"Do either of you know any editors of a daily paper? If so, write to such, draw attention to these expositions, urge your editors to come. Oh, if only we could capture the daily press! What an extended pulpit, what a far-reaching voice would our subject immediately possess!

"I don't quite know how far I ought to go on this line, but even as I speak, it comes to me to ask you if any one here present is acquainted with the evidently-gifted, open-minded editor of 'The Courier.' We have all,˙ of course, been struck by his own utterances from the 'Prophet's Chamber' column. Oh that he could be captured for Christ; then his paper would doubtless be a clarion for his Lord!"

Tom Hammond turned hot and cold. He trusted that no one had recognized him. He would be glad to get away unrecognized. Yet he was not offended by the speaker's personal allusion to him. He felt that the major's soul rang true.

"Before I close," the major went on, "suffer me to read an extract from the 'Gentleman's Magazine,' of the year seventeen hundred and fifty-nine:

"'Mr. Urban,—Reading over chapter eleven, verse two, of Revelation, a thought came to me that I had hit upon the meaning of it which I desire you'll publish in one of your future magazines. The verse runs thus:

"But the court which is without the temple leave out, and measure it not, for it is given to the Gentiles, and the holy city shall they tread under foot forty and two months."

" 'Now, according to the Scriptural way of putting a day for a year, if we multiply forty-two months by thirty (the number of days contained in a Jewish month,) we have the time the Turks will reign over the Jews' country, and the city of Jerusalem—viz., 1,260; which, if we add to the year of our Lord 636, when Jerusalem was taken by the Turks, we have the year of our Lord 1896, near or about which time the Jews will be reinstated in their own country and city, Jerusalem, again, which will be about 137 years hence; and that the Turks are the Gentiles mentioned in the above-quoted chapter and verse appears from their having that country and city in possession about 1,123 years, and will continue to possess it till the Omnipotent God, in His own time, bringeth this prophecy to its full period.'

"This letter is signed 'M. Forster,' and is dated from 'Bessborough, October 24th, 1759.' I have very little sympathy with those of our brethren who are ever venting in speech and in print the exact dates (as they declare) of the coming events surrounding the return of our Lord, but I do believe (in spite of the somewhat hazy chronology at our command) that the regarding of approximate times is perfectly permissible, and the letter I have read you has some value when, taking dates, etc., approximately, we remember that this letter was written nearly a hundred and fifty years ago, and that 1896 was memorable for a distinct movement towards the Holy Land.

"So, I say, 'the coming of the Lord draweth nigh.

To myself and to every Christian here, I would say, 'May God help us to quicken all our hearts, and purify all our lives, that we may not be ashamed at His coming.'

"And to any who are here (if such there be) who are not converted, may God help you to seek His face, that you may not be 'left,' when He shall suddenly, silently snatch away His Church out of this godless generation. 'Left!'

"Think of what that will mean, unsaved friend, if you are here to-day. Left! Left behind! When the Spirit of God will have been taken out of the earth. When Satan will dwell on the earth—for, with the coming of Christ into the air, Satan, 'the prince of the power of the air,' will have to descend.

"Christ and Satan can never live in the same realm. Oh, God, save anyone here from being left—left behind, to come upon the unspeakable judgments which will follow the taking out of the world of the Church!

"Some husband, whose head was laid on his bed,
  Throbbing with mad excess,
Awakes from that dream by the lightning gleam,
  Alone in his last distress.

"For the patient wife, who through each day's life,
  Watched and wept for his soul,
Is taken away, and no more shall pray,
  For the judgment thunders roll.

"And that thoughtless fair who breathed no prayer,
  Oft as her husband knelt,
Shall find he is fled, and start from her bed
  To feel as never she felt.

"The children of day are summoned away;
  Left are the children of night.

"It is high time for us all to awake. God keep us

awake and watching for our Lord, for His precious name's sake. Amen."

The murmured Amens rolled through the congregation like the deep surge of a sea billow on a shingle shore.

"Our time has gone, friends," cried the major. "We will sing two verses only of the closing hymn 410, the first and last verse. Sing straight away."

Tom Hammond, wondered at it all much as ever, listened while the song rang out:

> "When Jesus comes to reward His servants,
>   Whether it be noon or night,
>   Faithful to Him will He find us watching?
>   With our lamps all trimmed and bright?
>
> CHORUS.
>
>   Oh, can we say we are ready, brother?
>   Ready for the soul's bright home?
>   Say, will He find you and me still watching,
>   Waiting, waiting, when the Lord shall come?
>
> "Blessed are those whom the Lord finds watching
>   In His glory they shall share:
>   If He shall come at the dawn or midnight,
>   Will He find us watching there?"

Again the chorus rang out, and as Tom Hammond left the hall, the question of it clung to him. It forced itself upon his brain; it groped about for his heart; it clamoured to be hearkened to.

CHAPTER XVI.

HER CABIN COMPANION.

"THERE'LL be one other lady with you in your cabin, miss."

The berth-steward's announcement in no way disconcerted Madge Finisterre. She had had two cabin companions on the outward voyage.

She was arranging her cabin necessaries when her fellow-traveller entered. She was a wee, winsome girl, very fragile in appearance, with a yearning sweetness in her great grey eyes, such as Madge had never seen in any eyes before. With half-a-dozen words of exchanged greeting and a very warm handshake, the pair became instant friends.

By a strange but happy coincidence neither of them ever suffered from sea-sickness, and from the first moment of the great liner's departure they became inseparable.

As the vessel forged her way down Channel that evening, a glorious moon shining down upon them, the two girls, arm-in-arm, paced the promenade deck talking. The subject of the acute distress among the poor and out-of-works in all the world's great cities came up between them.

"Oh, if only our Lord would come quickly!" cried the girl—Kate Harland was her name.

"What do you mean, Kate?" Madge's voice was full of amazed wonder.

"I mean that——"

The fragile girl paused; then, glancing quickly up into Madge's face, she cried:

"You love Jesus, of course, Madge? You are saved, dear, and looking for His coming?"

For an instant Madge was silent. Then, with a deep sigh, she replied:

"Oh, me! I am afraid I am not saved, as you call it. Katie, dear, the fact is——"

She halted in her speech. She did not know how to put into words all that her friend's question had aroused within her.

While she halted thus, the girl at her side put her arms about her, clasping her with a kind of yearning —an "I will not let you go" kind of clasp—as she cried, softly:

"Oh, my darling, you must not lie down to-night until you know you are Christ's. Then—then—after that, nothing can ever matter. Come weal, come woe, come life, come death, all is well!"

*   *   *   *   *   *   *

It was past midnight before the two girls climbed into their berths, but by that time Madge Finisterre knew that she had passed from death into life.

Before the vessel reached New York she had learned something of the truth of the near return of the Lord.

On the quay, when they landed, the two girls bade each other a sorrowful farewell.

"We shall meet in heaven, Katie, if nevermore on earth," sobbed Madge.

"In the air, my darling," replied the other. "Do not let us lose sight of that. When our Lord shall come,

'Loved ones shall meet in a joyful surprise,
Caught up together to Him in the skies,
When Jesus shall come once again.' "

Kate Harland's friends, who had travelled to meet her from Denver, carried her off, and Madge took the car to the Central.

One hour later she boarded the train and began the last lap of her long journey.

Her spirits rose higher every moment. She had conceived a very bold idea, and she was going to carry it through after her own fashion. She sent no message of warning of her coming, as this would spoil her little plot.

Her eyes rested delightedly upon every place she passed. At Garrisons, where the train waited a few minutes, she caught a glimpse of the father of the man whom she was hurrying to meet.

The white-haired old father lived at Garrisons, and was a preacher of the Gospel, like his son. He was leaving the depot as her train pulled up. She easily recognized him, because several times during his son's pastorate at Balhang he had been to see him, staying a week at a time, and preaching once on the Sunday on each occasion.

At Duchess Junction she had to change trains. To her joy, she met no one from Balhang; there was not a soul at the depot whom she even knew by sight.

Just before her train reached Balhang she donned a thick brown gauze veil. No one could see her face through this to recognize it. There would be nothing to detain her at the depot, for her baggage was all "expressed."

The train stopped; she alighted. Several people

peered hard at her, the depot manager especially, as he took her check, but no one recognized her. She passed on. Twenty yards from the depot she met Judge Anstey.

She stopped him with a "Good day, Judge; can I speak with you?"

"Certainly, madam," the official replied genially.

"Come aside, Judge," she whispered. "I don't want anyone to recognize me, or to hear what I am saying to you, should people pass."

As he moved on by her side in the direction she wished, she whispered:

"I have put on this thick veil, Judge, so as not to be recognized. I am Madge Finisterre."

"Du say!" he gasped. "I knew the voice, but could not recall whose it was. I hadn't heard a breath of your coming home, Miss Madge."

"I let no one, not even mumma and poppa, know that I was coming," she replied. "The fact is, Judge——"

She was glad, as she prepared to take him into her confidence, that the thick veil would hide the hot colour that she felt leaped into her face.

"Momma wrote me," she went on, "that the pastor was very sick, and that the doctor didn't understand his case. I only got the letter last Saturday morning. The boat was to start that day at two; but I caught it, for I knew that would cure the pastor."

She felt how fiercely the blushes burned in her cheeks, but, assured that he could not see them, she went on:

"Just before I started for Europe, Judge, pastor told me he loved me, and asked me to be his wife——"

She watched the amused amaze leap into the Judge's face, and smiled herself at his low whistle.

"I told him," she continued, "I could make him no definite promise, as I was not quite sure of myself; but that, when I was, I would not wait for him to ask me again—I would come and tell him. I am going straight to him now, Judge, and I want you to give me a clear quarter of an hour's start. While I am gone to fix him up and to make him happy, I want you to go 'long to mumma and poppa, and bring them right along with you, and marry me and pastor as soon as you git up to us. So-long for a quarter of an hour."

Without another word she moved swiftly away.

"She's tropical!" he laughed, as he saw her making for Mrs. Keller's, where the pastor boarded.

* * * * * *

The French windows of the pastor's sitting-room were open, for the day was like a spring one. Madge moved quickly across the patch of grass, mounted the stoop, and peered in.

In a large rocker, looking very frail and ill, the young pastor was lying back with his eyes closed.

Madge felt her eyes fill with tears. She lifted the disguising veil, and wiped the salt drops away. She did not lower her veil again, but with a little glad cry of—

"Homer, dear love!" she crossed the threshold, and dropped on her knees by his side, flung her arms around his neck, and laid her hot lips to his.

It was like a dream to him—a wondrous, delicious dream. His thin arms clasped her. His kisses were rained upon her, but at first he found no words to say. Between their passionately-exchanged kisses she poured out, in rapid, caress-punctured speech, how she came to be there.

"I have not seen mumma or poppa yet," she explained; "but I met Judge Anstey down by the depot. I have sent him home for mumma and poppa; they will be here in no time now. The Judge will come with them, and will marry us right off, dear. For, say, you do want some nursing."

He found his voice at last, declared that her coming, her first kiss, had made him strong; that he would need no nursing now that she had come. Getting on to his feet, he gathered her into his arms, and rained fresh kisses upon her lips, her cheeks, her brow, her eyes.

She managed to whisper the good news, "I have found Jesus, dear, or He found me, and now——"

A sound of voices and of hurrying steps outside checked her. She had only time to tear herself from his arms when her mother and father reached her side.

An hour later, when the Judge had been and gone again, Madge Finisterre was the wife of the pastor.

CHAPTER XVII.

CASTING A SHOE.

IT was two hours after midnight when Tom Hammond was free at last. But he did not go to bed. His soul was disturbed. What he had heard at the major's meeting had stirred a myriad disquieting thoughts within him, and now that he was clear to do it, he shut himself up alone with a Bible, and began to go over every point of the major's address. He had taken copious notes in shorthand, paying especial attention to the texts quoted and referred to.

At the end of an hour he looked up from his Bible. There was a wondering amaze in his eyes, a strange, perplexed knitting of his brows.

"It is all most marvellous!" he murmured. "There is not a flaw or hitch anywhere in the major's statements or reasoning. The Scriptures prove, to the hilt, every word that he uttered."

He smiled to himself as, rising to his feet, he said aloud,

"I should not sleep if I went to bed; I will go out."

There are ways of getting into some of the London parks before the regulation hour for opening the gates. Tom Hammond had often found a way to forestall the park-opener.

Ten minutes after leaving his chambers he was inside the park he loved best. Everything was eerily still and silent. The calm suited his mood. He wanted to feel, as well as to be, absolutely alone. He had his desire.

There had been a thick mist over London overnight, but the atmosphere was as clear as a bell now. The air was as balmy as a morning in May or September.

There was a faint light from the stars that stabbed the deep violet sky. He moved slowly, thoughtfully, through paths as familiar to him as the rooms he occupied at home.

"And the Christ might come to-day!" he mused. "As Major H—— showed plainly from the Bible, there is no other prophetic event to transpire before His coming."

Almost unconsciously he paused in his walking.

"If," he cried softly, a certain fearsomeness in his voice, "if He came to-day, came now, what about me? Where should I come in?"

He recalled the fact that, according to the major's showing, he, Tom Hammond, was quite unprepared for Christ's coming, because he was still unsaved. He shivered slightly as the thought of his unpreparedness came to him.

With the flashing swiftness of one of memory's freaks, there leaped into his mind some lines of Charles Wesley's. He had written them, a day or two before, in illustration of a certain statement in an article on hymnology. They had not borne any message to his soul then, but now they seemed like the voicing of his own inmost thoughts.

He walked slowly on, the words falling from his lips in half-uttered notes.

> "And am I only born to die?
> And must I suddenly comply
>   With nature's stern decree?
> What after death for me remains—
> Celestial joys, or bitter pains,
>   To all eternity?

> "No room for mirth or trifling here,
> For worldly hope, or worldly fear,
>   If life so soon is gone—
> If now the Judge is at the door,
> And all mankind must stand before
>   The inexorable throne!

> "Nothing is worth a thought beneath,
> But how I may escape the death
>   That never, never dies—
> How make my own election sure,
> And, when I fail on earth, secure
>   A mansion in the skies."

"There was something inspiring, something helpful, in the last verse," he mused, "but, for the life of me, I cannot recall it."

The piping note of a robin from a clump of bush trees close by broke into his reverie. He lifted his head sharply and looked around, then upwards. The stars had paled in the violet dome above him. Somewhere near, ahead of him, was a piece of ornamental water. He caught a glimpse of it between the trees.

"Pip-pip!" came again from the robin's throat. He remembered Charles Fox, and said softly aloud:

> "Came forward to be seen,
> My little bright-eyed fellow,
> And an honest one as well O)
> In thy suit of olive green,
> With red-orange vest between,
> And small touching voice so mellow."

The bird suddenly flew across his path, dropped upon a low piece of iron fencing, glanced askance at him, then darted to where a morning meal peeped out of the damp sod.

Two or three other low, sleepy bird-notes followed, then the water-fowl began their discordant quacking. The tremulous flutenotes of a thrush made rich music on the morning air.

The stars faded out of sight. The cold grey light of dawning day moved into the eastern horizon. The smell of the earth grew rank. The air grew keener. The east slowly reddened. Roofs and towers of houses and churches grew up slowly, and grey amid the cold light of the dawn. He turned to face the spot where he knew the great clock-tower of Westminster could be seen. A light burned high aloft in the tower, telling that England's legislators were still in session.

Slowly, thoughtfully, he turned back to walk home.

"If Christ came at this instant," he mused, "how many of those Commoners and Peers would be ready to meet Him? And what of the teeming millions of this mighty city? God help us all! What blind fools we are!"

   *   *   *   *   *   *   *

In spite of his night vigil Tom Hammond was in his office at his usual hour. He had been there about an hour when there came a short, sharp rap on the panel of his room-door. In response to his "Come in!" Joyce, the drunken reporter lurched in. In some way he had contrived to elude those on duty in the enquiry-office.

He was the worse for drink, and in response to Hammond's sharp queries:

"What do you want? How came you here unannounced?" he began to "beg the loan of five shillings."

"Not a copper!" cried Hammond.

Joyce whined for it.

Hammond refused more sharply.

The drunken wretch cringed, whimpered for "just 'arf-a-crown."

The fellow began to bluster, then to threaten.

"If you don't leave this room, I'll hurl you out," cried Hammond, "and give you in custody of the police."

The drunken beast straightened his limp form as well as he was able, as he hiccoughed:

"All rightsh, Tom Ham'n'd. Every dawg hash hish day. You're havin' yoursh now, all rightsh—all rightsh, —but I'll—hic—do fur yer; I'll—hic—ruin yer; Ill——"

Tom Hammond darted from his place by the table. The next instant he would have put his threat of "hurling out" into execution, but the drunken braggart did not wait for him, for he shuffled out of the room, cursing hideously.

As the door closed upon him, Tom Hammond went across to the window, and flung up the lower sashes, and drew down the upper ones. From a drawer in a cabinet he took a strip of scented joss-paper, and lit it. The sandal-like perfume spread instantly through all the room.

"Faugh!" he muttered. "The whole place seems foul after his presence."

He turned to his wash-stand, rolled back the polished top, and washed his hands.

"I'll see Ralph, he muttered, as he dried his hands "and go out for a couple of hours. I'll go and see Cohen."

It was curious how often he found excuse to visit the Jew.

A quarter of an hour later he drove up to the house of Cohen. He found him, with his wife and Zillah, on the point of starting for their synagogue.

"One may live a life-time, as a Jew, in this country," Cohen explained, "and never see the ceremony that is about to take place in our synagogue. It is what is known in our religion as 'Chalitza.' Will you go with us, Mr. Hammond?"

Tom Hammond's eyes met Zillah's. Then he promptly said—

"Yes" to the Jew's question.

"Right, then! We can explain about the ceremony as we go!" Cohen said, and the quartette left the house.

There was not much time for explanation, but what Tom Hammond heard convinced him that he was a fortunate journalist that day. He had no opportunity of talking with Zillah, but he found his heart beating with a strange wildness whenever his eyes met hers—and they frequently met.

At the door of the synagogue tne party had to separate, the two women going one way, Cohen and Hammond another. The building was filling very fast. Presently it was packed to suffocation.

It was Tom Hammond's first sight of a Jewish congregation in a synagogue. It amazed him. The hatted men and bewigged women—these latter sat behind a grille. The gorgeousness of much of the female finery. The curious "praying shawls"—the "Talith" of the men.

Suddenly a Rabbi began to intone the opening words of the service, reading from the roll of the law, "The Holy Scroll:" "If brethren dwell together, and one of them die, and have no child, the wife of the dead shall not marry without unto a stranger; her husband's brother shall take her to wife, and perform the duty of a husband's brother to her. . . . And if the man like not to take his brother's wife, then let his brother's wife go up to the gate unto the elders, and say, My husband's brother refuseth to raise up unto his brother a name in Israel, he will not perform the duty of my husband's brother.

"Then the elder of the city shall call the man, and

speak unto him: and if he stand to it, and say, I like not to take her;

"Then shall his brother's wife come unto him in the presence of the elders, and loose his shoe from off his foot, and shall spit in his face, and shall answer and say. 'So shall it be done unto that man that will not build us his brothers' house.'

"And his name shall be called in Israel, 'the house of him that hath his shoe loosed'."

The service was all very curious in the eyes of Tom Hammond. He followed every item of it with the closest, most interested attention. Presently the parties specially concerned mounted the platform. This platform was backed with a huge square frame covered with black cloth. This was meant to symbolize mourning for the dead husband. Three tall candle-sticks held lighted candles, their flames looking weird and sickly in the daylight.

The Rabbi stooped before the brother-in-law, and took off his right shoe and sock. Another official washed the foot, wiped it with a towel, and pared the toe-nails.

A soft white shoe, made specially for the occasion, was then taken by the rabbi, put on to the bare foot of the man, and laced up very tightly, the long ends of the lace being twisted round the ankle and knotted securely.

Then there followed a seemingly interminable string of questions, put by the rabbi, and answered by the brother-in-law. The catechism culminated in a few chief questions such as:

"Do you wish to marry this woman?"

"I do not," replied the brother-in-law.

"For what reason?"

"I am already married; my wife is living, and the

law of the land we live in does not permit my having more than one wife.

The reply rang clear and strong through the silent building, and the hush seemed to deepen as the rabbi asked,

"Will you give this woman Chalitza?"

"Certainly I will, if she wishes it," replied the brother-in-law.

Turning to the woman, the rabbi asked, "Do you wish to receive Chalitza?"

Tom Hammond saw how the light of a great eagerness leaped into the eyes of the beautiful Jewess, and how her face glowed with the warmth of a sudden colour, as she replied,

"I do wish for Chalitza, for I desire to marry again."

The rabbi's assistant gave her certain instructions, and she knelt before her brother-in-law, and with the thumb and finger of her right hand—she dare not use the left, however difficult her task might prove,—she began untying the knots in the lace fastenings around the ankle.

It was no child's play to unfasten the shoe. The knots had been drawn very tight; but she was very determined, and presently a deep sigh of relief broke from the breathless, watching congregation, as, taking the shoe from the man's foot, she flung it sharply down, twice, upon the floor.

She rose now to her feet to complete the ceremony. The law of spitting in the face of the man had been modified to meet the views of a day less gross than when it was carried out in full coarseness.

The brother-in-law took a couple of paces backwards, and the beautiful widow spat on the place he had stood a moment before.

Then she faced the great congregation. Her eyes travelled straight to the face of the man she loved, whom she was shortly to marry. Her eyes danced with excitement, her cheeks were rosy with colour, her whole face was full of an indescribable rapture, as she cried:

"I am free!"

"True, sister, you are free!" the brother-in-law responded.

The rabbi moved swiftly to her side, and, looking into her face, said:

"O woman of Israel, you are free!"

With a shout that reminded Tom Hammond of the shout, "He is risen!" at the Easter service in the Greek churches of Russia, the excited, perspiring congregation cried: "Woman, you are free!"

A moment or two later the service concluded, and the building emptied. Walking homeward by Hammond's side, Cohen said, "Only the most orthodox of Jews would dream of using Chalitza to free themselves for re-marrying. This is the only case I have personally known. By-the-bye, Mr. Hammond, it is said that about the middle of the eighteenth century that one of the Rothschild widows sought Chalitza, but failed to untie the lace of the shoe, and was disqualified from re-marrying."

Cohen's wife had stopped to speak to some friends. The young Jew joined her. Tom Hammond found himself moving forward by Zillah's side.

"What an extraordinary service that was, Miss Robart!" he said.

"It was!" she glanced almost shyly away from him, for, unknown to himself his eyes were full of the warmest admiration.

"Do you think, Miss Robart," he went on, "if you

were situated as was that beautiful woman whom we have just seen freed from the Mosaic bond, that you would have braved the Chalitza ceremony, or would you have taken advantage of the English law and——"

She lifted her great, black, lustrous eyes to his in a sudden gaze of utter frankness, as, interrupting him, she cried:

"I would certainly not marry any man, save one whom I could wholly revere and love!"

"Happy the man whom you shall thus honour, Miss Robart!"

Tom Hammond barely whispered the words, and she was not wholly sure that he meant them for her ears. She did not respond in any way. But she was conscious that his gaze was fixed upon her. She was equally conscious that she was blushing furiously.

Perhaps it was to give her a chance of recovering herself, that his next question was on quite a different topic.

"Are you, Miss Robart," he said, "wholly wedded to the Jewish faith? Do you believe, for instance, that Jesus, the Nazarene, was an impostor?"

He heard the catch that came into her throat. Then, with a half-frightened look around, she lifted her melting eyes to his, as she said, "I can trust you, Mr. Hammon, I know. You will keep my confidence, if I give it to you?"

His eyes answered her, and she went on.

"I have not dared to breathe a word of it to anyone, not even to my good brother-in-law Abraham, but I am learning to love the Christ."

Her face was filled with a holy light, her cheeks glowed with excitement, as she went on:

"I see how the prophecies of our forefathers—Isaiah especially—were all literally fulfilled in the life and work of Jesus of Nazareth. I see, too, that when next He comes, it will not be as our race supposes, as the Messiah to the Jews, but He will come in the air, and——"

She glanced sharply round. Some instinct told her her friends were coming.

"No more now," she whispered. "I will tell you more another time. I shall myself know more, to-night. I go twice a week to a mission-room at Spitalfields——"

"What time?" he asked eagerly.

"Seven," she replied, not realizing the eagerness of his tone.

"Where is this place?" he went on.

She had just time to tell him. When Cohen and his wife came up, husband and wife began talking together. Zillah appeared to listen, but in reality she heard nothing of what they were saying. For a strange thing had happened.

She had dropped her hand by her side as the Cohens had rejoined them, and had suddenly found her fingers clasped in Hammond's hand.

What did it mean? she wondered. They had met often of late. She had read an unmistakable ardency in his eyes very often, when her glance met his. And, deep in her own heart, she knew that all the woman-love she would ever have to give a man she had unconsciously given to him. Was this sudden secret handclasp of his a silent expression of love on his part, or was it meant merely as an assurance of sympathy in the matter of her new faith?

She could not be sure which it was, but she let her plump fingers give a little pressure of response. How did he translate this response? she wondered. She had no means of deciding, save that her heart leaped wildly in a tumultous delight as she felt how he literally gripped her fingers in a closer, warmer clasp.

They had reached the house by this time. Hammond would not go in. He shook hands, in parting, with each, but his hold upon Zillah's hand was longer than on the others. He pressed the fingers meaningly, and his eyes held an ardency that gave a new tumult to her heart.

As she passed into the house she whispered to herself, "Will he be at Spitalfields to-night?"

CHAPTER XVIII.

TOLD IN A CAB.

A QUARTER of an hour before the time Zillah had given him, Tom Hammond was waiting near the "Mission Hall for Jews," where the meeting was to be held. He was anxious that she should not know of his proximity, so kept out of sight,—there were many possibilities of this among the various stalls in the gutter-way.

Presently he saw her coming, and the light of a glad admiration leaped into his eyes. "What a superb face and figure she has!" he mused. "What a perfect queen of a woman she is!"

From behind a whelk-stall he watched her cross over to the door of the Hall. Here she paused a moment, and glanced around.

"I believe she half expected to see me somewhere near!" he murmured to himself.

She entered the Hall. By the time her head was bowed in prayer, he had entered, and had taken a seat on the last form, the fourth behind hers. When she first raised her head from her silent prayer, she looked around and backward. In her heart she was hoping he would be there. If he had not been bending in prayer, she must have seen him. After that she turned no more, the service soon occupied all her thoughts.

He too became utterly absorbed by the service, of which the address was the chief feature. It was largely expository, and from the first utterance of the speaker, it riveted Tom Hammond's attention.

The speaker, himself a converted Jew, took as his text Deut. xxi. 22, 23.

"If a man have committed a sin worthy of death, and is sentenced to death, and thou hang him on a tree, his corpse shall not remain all night upon the tree, but, burying, thou shalt bury him on that day (because he who is hanged is accursed of God.")

"Now, brethren," the speaker went on, "as far as I have been able to discover, in all the Hebrew records I have been able to consult, and in all the histories of our race, I have not found a single reference to a Hebrew official hanging of a criminal on a tree. To what, then, does this verse refer, and why is it placed on Jehovah's statute-book?"

For a few moments he appealed to his Jewish hearers on points peculiarly Hebraic. Then presently he said,

"Now let us see if the New Testament will shed any light upon this."

Turning rapidly the leaves of his Bible, he went on: "There is a book in the Christian Scriptures known as the Epistle to the Galatians which, in the tenth verse of the third chapter, repeats our own word from Deuteronomy:

"Cursed is every one that continueth not in all things which are written in the Book of the Law to do them,' and in the thirteenth verse says, 'Christ hath redeemed us from the curse of the law, being made a curse for us: for it is written, Cursed is every one that hangeth on a tree.'

"We all, brethren, as the sons of Abraham, believe that our father David's Psalm beginning, 'My God, my God, why hast Thou forsaken me?' was never written out of his own experience, but was prophetic of some other Person. Now, let me quote you some of the words of that Psalm."

In clear, succinct language, the speaker, quoting verse after verse of the Psalm, showed how literally the descriptions fitted into a death by crucifixion. Referring to the Gospel narratives of the death on the cross, he showed how they also fitted in with the description of Christ's death, and how Christ actually took upon His dying lips the cry of the Psalm, "My God, My God, why hast Thou forsaken Me?"

Then with wondrous clearness he referred to parts of Isaiah liii., and, continuing his theme, showed that it was evident that only one particular type of death could have atoned for the sin of the human race, a death that would render the dying one accursed of the Almighty. The only death that would fully carry out that condition was crucifixion.

"Our race waited for the Messiah," he cried, "and He came. Our prophet Micah said, 'Yet thou, O Bethlehem-Ephratah, little as thou art amidst the thousands of Judah, yet out of thee shall proceed from Me, One who is to be ruler in Israel!'

"The Christ was born at the only time in the world's history when He could have been executed on a tree—crucified. At a time when the Roman—crucifixion was a Roman punishment—swayed our beloved land of Jewry. So that Paul, the great Jew, chosen of God to be apostle to the Gentiles, wrote after the crucifixion of Jesus, the Nazarene, 'According to the time, Christ died."

For some minutes the speaker appealed to his Jewish hearers with a wonderful power. Then finally addressing not only the Jews, but any Gentiles who might be present, he cried:

"We must know the meaning of sin, brethren, before we can understand the mystery of a crucified Christ. A beheaded, a stoned Christ, could not have atoned for a guilty world, but only a God-cursed death, a tree-cursed death could have done this.

"And Christ was cursed for us—He who knew no curse of His own. Ah! beloved, the guilt of the human race is the key to the cross.

"Times change, customs change, but sin remains, sin is ever the same, and only a living, personal trust in the crucified Christ can ever deliver the unsaved sinner from the wrath of God which abideth on him."

The address closed. Tom Hammond awoke from his intense absorption of soul. He had long since utterly forgotten Zillah. He had seen only himself, at first, his own sin, and that his sin had nailed Christ to the cross. Then, better still, he saw the Christ.

Only a few nights before he had paused to watch a Salvation Army open-air meeting. The girl-officer in charge of the corps had announced thirty-eight as the number of the hymn they would sing, and prefaced the reading of the first verse by saying:

"This hymn was written by an ex-drunkard—an ex-blasphemer. His name was Newton—drunken Jack Newton, he was often called by his mates, and by others who knew him. He was a sailor, on a ship trading to the African coast, at the time when his soul was aroused to its danger. He was in agony, not knowing what to do to get rest and peace.

"One night he was keeping anchor-watch. He was alone on the deck, the night was dark and eerie. His sins troubled him. All that he had heard of the crucified Christ—whom he had so often blasphemed—swept into his soul, and he groaned in the misery of his sin-convicted state.

"Suddenly he paused in his deck-pacing, and looked up. To his fevered imagination, the yard which crossed the mast high up above his head appeared like a mighty cross, and it was remembering this, with all the soul-experience of that night, that in after years, when he became a preacher of the gospel, and a noted divine, Dr. John Newton wrote:

> "I saw One hanging on a tree
>   In agonies and blood,
> Who fixed His dying eyes on me,
>   As near the cross I stood.
> 'A second look He gave, which said,
>   "I freely all forgive
> My blood was for thy ransom paid,
>   I die that thou may'st live.' " "

Recalling these words now, Tom Hammond's soul received the great Revelation. He heard no word of the closing hymn and prayer, but passed out into the open air a new man in Christ.

The mission-leader had given an invitation to any who would like to be helped in soul matters to remain behind. Tom Hammond noticed that Zillah lingered.

It was half-an-hour before she came out. Tom Hammond had lived a lifetime of wonder in the thirty minutes.

Like one in a delicious dream Zillah walked on a few vards. Suddenly she became aware of Tom Hammond's presence at her side.

"Zillah!"

He gave her no other word of greeting. It was the first time he had ever called the young girl by her first name. He took her hand, and drew it through his arm. She barely noticed the tender action, for her soul was rioting in a new-found joy, and she poured out, in a few sentences, all the story of her supreme trust in Christ the Nazarene.

His voice was hoarse with many emotions, as he said,

"I, too, Zillah, have to-night seen Jesus Christ dying for my sin, and have taken Him for my own personal Saviour!"

Suddenly she realized how closely he was holding her to his side, how tight was the clasp of his hand upon hers. She looked up into his face to express her joy at his new-found faith. Their eyes met. A new meaning flashed in their exchanged glances.

A four-wheeled cab moved slowly along in the gutter-way, the driver uttered a low "Keb, keb!"

Tom Hammond seized the opportune offer, and whispered,

"Let us take a cab, Zillah. I have something to say to you which I must say to-night."

Before scarcely she realized it, she was seated by his side in the cab.

There is a moment in every woman's life when her heart warns her of the coming of the great event in that life, when love is to be offered to her by the only man who has ever loomed large enough in her consciousness to be able to affect her existence.

This moment had suddenly unexpectedly come to Zillah Robart.

Her heart warned her that the crisis was upon her. She had done nothing to precipitate it. It had met her, drawn her aside, and had shut her up in the semi-darkness of this vehicle with the only man she could ever love.

The cab rattled over the cobbles of that wide East-end thoroughfare, past the throngs of moving pedestrians, though, to her consciousness, the whole wide world consisted of but one man—the man at her side.

He had secured her hand, he held it in his strong, hot clasp. She held her breath in a strange, expectant ecstasy. Then the inevitable came. She felt its coming.

Tom Hammond was drawing her closer to himself. She was yielding to that drawing. She caught her breath again, and as she did so a rush of strange tears filled her eyes.

"Zillah!" his voice was hoarse and deep.

She realized the meaning of the hoarseness. She knew by her own feeling that the depth and intensity of his voice was due to the emotion that filled him. She knew she would have found herself voiceless at that moment had she tried to speak.

"I love you, my darling!" he went on. "I have loved you from the first instant I met you. You have felt it, known it, dear. Have you not?"

She tried to speak, her lips moved, but no sound came from them. But she looked into his eyes, and he read his answer.

With a sweeping gesture of passionate love he gathered her into his arms and showered kisses upon her lips, her cheeks, her forehead, her hair.

She lay like a stunned thing in his arms. Her joy was almost greater than she could bear. Then as his hot lips sought hers again, she awoke from her semi-trance of ecstasy, and with a little sob she flung her arms upwards and clasped them about his neck, crying,

"Love you, my darling? Love seems too poor a word to express my feeling, for God knows that, save my

Lord Jesus, to whom to-night I have fully yielded, you are all my life."

Her voice was stifled with a little rush of tears. Where she lay on his breast, he felt how all her frame quivered.

"And you will be mine, dear Zillah—and soon?" His eyes burned into hers, asking for an answer as loudly as his lips.

She did not answer him for a moment. Her heart beat with a tumultuous gladness, and her brain throbbed with the wonder of what she conceived to be the honour that had come to her. Wondering incredulity mingled with the rapturous ecstasy that filled her.

"But you are so great—so——" She paused, she could find no words to express all that prospective wifedom to him appeared to her.

He smiled down into her eyes. Her loveliness seemed to him greater than ever before.

"You seem like a king to me!" she gasped at last.

"You, Zillah," he smiled, "do not seem, you are, a queen to me. Say, darling, the one word that shall fill all my soul with delight—say that you will be mine —and soon, very soon!"

"I will."

There was the intensity of a mighty love in her utterance of the two words.

He gathered her to himself in an even closer embrace, and spent his kisses on her lips.

The flush of pride, of love, burned deeper in her face.

"Oh, why is it given to me to have such bliss?" she murmured.

The words were low-breathed; they sounded like a gasping sigh of delight more than a voiced utterance.

For a moment, clasped tightly in his arms, she was

silent, and he uttered no word. Presently he whispered,

"Will it give you joy, I wonder, my darling, to know that I have been a man free of all woman's love before? I have seen many women, in many lands, the loveliest of the earth—though none so lovely as you, my sweetheart. It is no egotism on my part, either, to say that many women have sought my love by their smiles and favour. But none ever won a word of love or response from me."

The cab was passing a great central light in the heart of a junction of four roads. Her eyes, full of a great rapture, sought his. His were fixed upon her face, and filled with a love so great that again she caught her breath in wonder.

"But you, my Zillah!" He caught her close to himself again, and bending his head, let his lips cling to hers, "But you, darling!" he continued, "have been to me all that the heart of man could ever wish for, from the first moment I met you. May God give us a long life together, dearest, and make us (with our new-born faith in Him) to be the best, the holiest help-meets, the one to the other, that this world has ever known."

Where she lay in his arms, he felt her tremble with the intensity of her joy. As he looked down into the deep, dreamy lustrousness of her eyes, he saw how they were full of a far-off look, as though she was picturing that united future of which he had spoken.

Perhaps he read that look in her eyes aright. Then, as he watched her, he saw how the colour deepened in her face. She slowly, proudly, yet with a glad frankness, lifted herself in his arms until, in a tender, passionate caress, her lips rested upon his in the first spontaneous kiss she had given him.

"If the Christ, to whom we have given ourselves to-night, should tarry," she whispered, "and we are spared to dwell together on earth as husband and wife, dear Tom, may God answer all that prayer of yours abundantly."

The cab turned a corner sharply at that moment. He looked through the window. They were within a few hundred yards of where he had given the driver orders to stop. Zillah would have, on alighting, only the length of a short street to traverse before reaching home, and he would take a hansom and drive back to the office. But the intervening moments before they would part were very precious, and love took unlimited toll in those swift, fleeting moments.

CHAPTER XIX.

TOM HAMMOND REVIEWING.

IT was the morning after Tom Hammond had found Christ, and had closed with the great offer of redemption. He had scarcely slept for the joy of the two loves that had so suddenly come into his life.

During the sleepless hours, he had learned, for the first time in his life, the true secret of prayer, and that even greater secret, that of communion.

With real prayer there is always a certain degree of communion, but real, deep, soul-filling communion is more often found in seasons when the communing one asks for nothing, but, silent before his or her God, the sense of the Divine fills all the being, and if the lips utter any sound it is the cry, "My Lord and my God!"

Tom Hammond, reviewing all that God had revealed to him, learned in those first hours of his new birth the secret of adoring communion with God.

In the book of extracts he had been reading in the tube train at the moment when he had first heard of Major H——'s coming address on the Second Advent, he had come across one headed, "Frederick William Faber: The Precious Blood—chap. iv." He had at the time been considerably impressed with the extract, though there was a certain note about it which he had failed to understand. In the flush of the great revelation that had come to his soul (in that little meeting at Spitalfields), he now found the book, and re-read the extract:

"I was upon the sea-shore; and my heart filled with love it knew not why. Its happiness went out over the wide waters, and upon the unfettered wind, and swelled up into the free dome of blue sky until it filled it. The dawn lighted up the faces of the ivory cliffs, which the sun and sea had been blanching for centuries of God's unchanging love. The miles of noiseless sands seemed vast, as if they were the floors of eternity. Somehow, the daybreak was like eternity. The idea came over me of that feeling of acceptance which so entrances the soul just judged and just admitted into heaven.

"'To be saved!' I said to myself, 'to be saved!'

"Then the thoughts of all the things implied in salvation came in one thought upon me; and I said:

"'This is the one grand joy of life;' and I clapped my hands like a child, and spoke to God aloud. But then there came many thoughts, all in one thought, about the nature and manner of our salvation. To be saved with such a salvation!

"This was a grander joy, the second grand joy of life; and I tried to say some lines of a hymn but the words were choked in my throat. The ebb was sucking the sea down over the sand quite silently; and the cliffs were whiter, and more day-like. Then there came many more thoughts all in one thought, and I stood still without intending it.

"To be saved by such a Saviour! This was the grandest joy of all, the third grand joy of life; and it swallowed up the other joys; and after it there could be on earth no higher joy.

"I said nothing; but I looked at the sinking sea as it reddened in the morning. Its great heart was throbbing in the calm; and methought I saw the precious blood of Jesus in heaven, throbbing that hour with real human love of me."

"Yes," murmured Tom Hammond, "after all, to be saved by such a Saviour is a greater, higher, holier thought than the mere knowledge that one is saved, or of the realization of what that salvation comprises."

In every way that night was one never to be forgotten by Tom Hammond. He needed, too, all the strength born of his new communion with God to meet what awaited him with the coming of the new day's daily papers.

The paper from whose staff he had been practically dismissed in our first chapter (the editor of which was his bitterest enemy) had found how to use "the glass stiletto."

Some of the most scurrilous paragraphs ever penned appeared in his enemy's columns that morning. It is true that the identity of the man slandered (Tom Hammond) was veiled, but so thinly—so devilishly—that every journalist, and a myriad other readers, would know against whom the scurrilous utterances were hurled.

Tom Hammond would not have been human if the reading of the paragraphs had not hurt him. And he would not have been "partaker of the Divine nature," as he now was, if he had not found a balm in the committal of his soreness to God.

"That is the work of that fellow Joyce," he told himself.

Twenty-four hours before, if this utterance had had to have been made by him, he would have said,

"That beast Joyce!" But already, as a young soldier of Christ, the promised watch was set upon his lips. In the strength of the two great loves that had come into his life—the love of Christ and the love of Zillah Robart

—the scurrilous paragraphs affected him comparatively little.

When he had skimmed the papers, attended to his correspondence, and to one or two other special items, he took pen and paper and began to write to his betrothed.

His pen flew over the smooth surface of the paper, but his thoughts were even quicker than his pen. His whole being palpitated with love. It was the love of his highest ideal. The love which he had sometimes dared to hope might some day be his, but which he had scarcely dared to expect.

The memory of his passing fancy for Madge Finisterer crossed his mind, once, as he wrote. He paused with the pen poised in his fingers, and smiled that he should ever have thought it possible that he was beginning to love her. "I liked her, admired her," he mused. "I enjoyed her frank, open friendship, but love her—no, no. The word cannot be named in the same breath as my feeling for Zillah."

He put his pen to the paper again, and poured out all the wealth of the love of his heart to his beautiful betrothed. When he had finally finished the letter, he sent it by special messenger to Zillah.

He had not forgotten that Major H——'s second meeting was that day. Three o'clock found him again in the hall. This time it was quite full. There was a new sense of interest, of understanding, present within him as he entered the place. This time he bowed his head in real prayer.

The preliminary proceedings were almost identically like those of the previous occasion, except that the hymn sung—though equally new to Hammond—was different to either of those sung at the first meeting. But, if anything, he was more struck by the words than he had been with those of the other hymns.

And how rapturously the people sang:

> "'Till He come!' Oh, let the words
> Linger on the trembling chords;
> Let the 'little while' between
> In their golden light be seen;
> Let us think how heaven and home
> Lie beyond that 'Till He come!'"

This time a lady, a returned Chinese missionary, led prayer, and then the major resumed his subject.

"We saw, dear friends, at our last meeting," the grand old soldier-preacher began, "what were some of the prophesied signs of our Lord's second coming and how literally these signs were being fulfilled in our midst to-day. This afternoon, God willing, and time permitting, I want us to see how He will come; what will happen to the believer; and also what effect the expectancy of His coming should have upon us, as believers.

"First of all, how will He come? While Jesus, who had led His disciples out of the city, was in the act of blessing them, He suddenly rose before their eyes, and a cloud received Him out of their sight. Have you ever thought of this fact, beloved, that the cloud itself was a miracle? Whoever heard of a cloud at that special period of the year, in Palestine? And I very much doubt if anyone, save the apostles, in all the country round about, saw that cloud. If you ask me what I think the cloud was, I should be inclined to refer you to the 24th Psalm, and say that the cloud was composed of the angel-convoy, who, like a guard of honour, escorted the Lord back to glory, crying, as they neared the gates of the celestial city, 'Lift up your heads, oh, ye gates, and let the King of Glory come in!"

"He went away in a cloud. The angels, addressing the amazed disciples declared to them that 'He would so come in like manner as ye have seen Him go.'

"It may be that to the letter that will be fulfilled, and that our Lord's return for His Church will be in an actual cloud. I think it is probable it will. Anyway, we know that He will come 'in the air,' for Paul, to whom was given, by God, the privilege of revealing to His Church the great mystery of the second coming of our Lord, and who said, in this connection:

" 'Behold, I show you a mystery: we shall not all sleep, but we shall all be changed, in a moment, in the twinkling of an eye,' when writing more explicitly to the church at Thessalonica, said:

" 'For this we say unto you by the word of the Lord, that we which are alive and remain unto the coming of the Lord shall not prevent them which are asleep. For the Lord Himself shall descend from heaven with a shout, with the voice of the archangel, and with the trump of God, and the dead in Christ shall rise first. Then we which are alive and remain shall be caught up together with them in the clouds, to meet the Lord in the air; and so shall ever be with the Lord. Wherefore comfort one another with these words.'

"Now, beloved, can any words be plainer, simpler, than these of Paul's, forming, as they do, the climax to all that has gone before in the New Testament. Jesus had Himself said,

" 'I will come again and receive you unto Myself.'

"The angels said,

" 'In like manner as ye have seen Him go, He shall come again,' and now Paul amplifies this manner of His coming, while, at the same time, he emphasizes the fact of that return.

"Now let us look, dear friends, at the separate items of that detailed coming. We have already, more than once, alluded to the secrecy of the return of our Lord for His people, and people are puzzled over the language used by Paul's description of the return. 'The Lord shall come with a shout.' Then the world at large will hear Him coming? No; we think not. Or, if they hear a sound, they will not understand it.

"The Lord's voice in His spiritual revelations is never heard save by the Lord's people. But there is the voice of the archangel—how about that? The same rule applies to that, we think.

"There were godly shepherds watching their flocks at night, near Bethlehem, and there was a whole host of angels singing, but the Bethlehemites did not hear. No one appears to have heard or seen anything save the godly shepherds. The same, we believe, applies to the 'trump,' the call of God.

"In this connection it is interesting to note a fact that probably was in the mind of Paul when he wrote thus to the Thessalonians. The Roman army used three special trumpet-calls in connection with departure—with marching.

"The first meant, 'Pull down tents.'

"The second, 'Get in array.'

"The third, 'Start.'

"Did Paul, moved by the Holy Ghost, translate these three clarion notes in the topic of 1 Thess. iv. 16, after this fashion:

"1. 'The Lord Himself.'

"2. 'Voice of the archangel.'

"3. 'The trump of God.'

"But leaving that, again I would emphasize this truth, that it is only the trained ear of the spiritually-awakened soul which ever hears the call of God. We believe that all Scripture teaches the secrecy as well as the suddenness of the rapture of the church.

"In all the many appearances of the risen, resurrected Lord Jesus, during the many weeks between the resurrection and the ascension, even though, on one occasion, at least, He was seen by 500 disciples at once, yet there is no hint, either in the Word of God or in the records of history of that time, that Jesus was ever seen by the eye of an unbeliever. And depend upon it, no eye will see, no ear will hear Him, when He comes again, save those who are in Christ.

" 'The world seeth Me no more' our Lord said, 'but ye see Me.' 'Him God raised up the third day, and gave Him to be made manifest, not to all the people, but unto witnesses that were chosen before God, even to us who did eat and drink with Him after He rose from the dead.'

"When the voice of the Father came from heaven, witnessing to Jesus' truth, the people that stood by failed to hear it as a voice, but exclaimed,—'It thunders.' In the case of Paul on the way to Damascus, those with him heard nothing understandable.

"Enoch was taken secretly. Noah was shut into the ark before the flood came. Only Israel, at Sinai, and not the surrounding nations, understood those awful physical manifestations of God's power. Elijah was

taken secretly. The nation neither saw nor heard anything of it.

"When will He come? I do not know; no one knows
exactly; but this we do know, from the Word of God—
that nothing remains to be fulfilled before He comes.
He may come before this meeting closes. Again we
know by every sign of the times that His coming can
not now be delayed much longer.

"Now to a very important feature as to the truth of
the second coming of the Lord. There are many who
argue that such teaching will tend to make the Christian
worker careless of his work, his life, etc. There was
never a more foolish argument advanced.

"First take a concrete illustration that gives the flat
denial to it—namely, that the most spiritual-minded
workers, at home and abroad, are those whose hearts
(not heads only) are saturated with, not the doctrine
merely, but the expectancy of their Lord's near return.
Then, too, every such worker finds an incentive to
redoubled service in the remembrance that every soul
saved through their instrumentality brings the Lord's
return nearer—'hasting His coming'—since, when the last
unit composing His Church has been gathered in, He will
come.

"Scripture, dear friends, is most plain, most emphatic,
in its statements that the effect of living in momentary
expectancy of our Lord's return touches the spiritual
life and service at every point. 'We know,' wrote John,
'that when He shall appear we shall be like Him, for we
shall see Him as He is. And every man that hath this
hope in him purifieth himself, even as He is pure.' That,
beloved, is the general statement. Now let us look at
some of the separate particular statement.

"Writing to the Philippians, Paul connects heavenly mindedness with the return of the Lord for His Church saying, 'For our conversation'—our manner of living, our citizenship—'is in heaven; from whence also we look for the Saviour, the Lord Jesus Christ.' To the Colossians the great apostle showed how the coming of the Lord was to be the incentive to mortification of self. 'When Christ, who is our life, shall appear, then shall ye also appear with Him in glory. Mortify, therefore, your members which are upon the earth,' etc. James taught that the real cure for impatience was this dwelling in the hope and expectancy of our Lord's coming again. 'Be ye also patient,' he wrote; 'stablish your hearts; for the coming of the Lord draweth nigh!' We live in an age which is cursed with impatience—children, young men and women, parents, business people, domestic people, pastors, Christian workers, Sunday-school teachers, all alike have their spiritual lives and their work marred by impatience. A real, moment-by-moment heart-apprehension of the possible coming of Jesus in the next moment of time, is the only real cure for this universal impatience in the Christian Church.

"Then take another great sin in the Church, beloved —censoriousness. Oh, the damage it does to the one who indulges in it, and the suffering it causes to the one who is the victim of it. But here, again, a full, a constant realization of the near coming of our Lord will check censoriousness. Writing to the Corinthians, in his first epistle, Paul says, 'Therefore, judge nothing before the time, until the Lord come, who both will bring to light the hidden things of darkness, and make manifest the counsels of the hearts.'

"The great quickener, too, of Christian diligence is to

be found in the coming of the Lord. Peter writes to us saying, 'But the day of the Lord will come as a thief in the night, . . . seeing then that these things shall be, . . . what manner of persons ought we to be in all holy living and godliness; looking for and hasting the coming. . . . Wherefore, beloved, seeing that ye look for such things, be diligent that ye may be found of Him in peace, without spot, and blameless.'

"May I say, too, in all gentleness and love, that it has seemed to me, for years, that the missing link in nearly all 'holiness' preaching (so called) is this much-neglected expectancy of our Lord's return. Paul connects holiness and the second coming of Christ, in his first epistle to the Thessalonians, saying, 'The God of peace sanctify you wholly; and I pray God your spirit, soul and body be preserved blameless unto the coming of our Lord Jesus Christ.'

"The scoff of the world, dear friends, against us, as Christians, is that the professed bond of love is absent from our life. And here again God's Word shows us that a real living in expectancy of our Lord's return would teach us to love one another. In that same epistle I have just quoted, Paul says, 'The Lord make you to increase and abound in love one toward another, and toward all men, even as we do toward you: to the end He may stablish your hearts unblameable in holiness before God, even our Father, at the coming of our Lord with all His saints.'

"I have only time, this afternoon, for but one more of these references, and that is a very elementary though a very essential one. Paul, in that same epistle, teaches that to be saved means that we are saved to serve. 'Ye turned to God,' he says, 'to serve . . . and to wait for His Son from heaven.'

"I must close, friends. But before I do, do let me beseech every Christian here this afternoon to go aside with God, and with His plain, unadulterated Word. Assure yourself that Jesus is coming again, that He is coming soon, and that you are so living that you shall 'not be ashamed at His coming.' Should He tarry till Thursday next, and He is willing to suffer me to meet you here again, we will continue this great subject on the line of the three judgments. Let us close our meeting by singing hymn number 308."

Like one in a strange, delicious dream, Tom Hammond rose with the others and sang:

> "Jesus is coming! Sing the glad word!
> Coming for those He redeemed by His blood,
> Coming to reign as the glorified Lord!
> Jesus is coming again!"

As he left the hall, and thought, "How Zillah would have enjoyed, how she would have been helped, by this meeting!" he muttered.

"How senseless of me not to have told her of it when I wrote this morning.

He smiled a little to himself as he murmured:

"May I take this bit of remissness as a sign that the Divine love was predominant within me, rather than the human? Or was it that I am not yet sufficiently taught in the school of human love?"

CHAPTER XIXA.

"MY MENTOR."

IT was about the hour that Tom Hammond entered the Hall to listen to the Major's second address. Cohen, the Jew, was in his workshop, his brain busy with many problems, while his hands wrought out that wondrous Temple work.

The door opened, quietly, and Zillah entered. She often came for a talk with him at this hour, as she was mostly sure of an uninterrupted conversation. Her sister, to a large extent, lived to eat, and always slept for a couple hours or more after her hearty two o'clock dinner.

The young Jew gave the beautiful girl a pleasant greeting. Then, after the exchange of a few very general words, the pair were silent. Zillah broke the silence at last.

"Abraham," she began, "I want to talk to you on— on—well— I've something important to say."

He eyed her curiously, a tender little smile moving about among the lines of his mouth. There was a new note in her voice, a new light in her eyes. He had caught glimpses of both when they had met at breakfast, and again at dinner, but both were more marked than ever now.

He had laid down his tool at her first word of address. Now she laid one of her pretty plump hands on his, as she went on :——

"You could not have been kinder, truer, dear Abraham, if you had been my own brother, *after the flesh*. I have looked upon you *as* a brother, as a friend, as a protector, and I have always felt that I could, and would make a confident of you, should the needs-be ever arise."

The gentle smile in his eyes as well as his mouth encouraged her, and she went on:—

"A gentleman has asked me to marry him, Abraham——"

Cohen gave a quick little start, but in her eagerness she did not notice it.

"I have promised," she continued, "for I love him, and he loves me as only——"

"Who is he, Zillah?"

"Mr. Hammond, dear!"

His eyes flashed with the mildest surprise. But, to her astonishment, she noticed that he showed no anger.

In spite of all his usual gentleness she had half expected a little outburst, for to marry *out* of the Jewish faith, was equal in shame almost to turning Meshumed, and usually brought down the curse of one's nearest and dearest.

"He is of the Gentile race, Zillah!" Cohen said quietly.

She noticed that he said *race*, and not *faith*, and she unconsciously took courage from the fact.

She was silent for a moment. Her lips moved slightly, but no sound came from her. Watching her, he wondered. She was praying!

Suddenly she lifted her head, proudly almost. She

suffered her great lustrous eyes,——liquid in their love light——to meet his, as she said, with a ringing frankness :——

"Abraham! I have found the Messiah! He whom the Gentiles call the Christ; The man-God, Jesus, *is* the Messiah!"

His eyes dwelt fixedly upon her face. She wondered that there was neither anger nor indignation in them.

"May I tell you why I think, why I *know* He is the Messiah, Abraham?" she asked.

"Do, Zillah!"

He spoke very gently, and she wondered more and more. She made no remark, however, on his toleration, but began to pour out her soul in the words of the Old Testament scriptures, connecting them with their fulfillment in the New Testament.

Cohen, watching her, thought of Deborah, for all her beautiful form seemed suddenly ennobled under the power of the theme that fired her.

"Now I know, dear Abraham," she presently cried, "How it is that Jehovah is allowing our Rabbis—you told me, you know, the other day, of the one at Safed— to be led to dates that prove that Messiah is coming soon? *Now* I know why God has allowed our nation to be stirred up,—the Zionist movement, the colonization of Jerusalem and its neighbourhood, and all else of this like—yes, it is because the Christ *is* coming.

"Only, dear brother, it is not as the Messiah of the Jews that He comes soon—He came thus more than 1,900 years ago—this time, when He comes, He will come for His church, His redeemed ones—Jew and Gentile alike who are washed in His blood that was shed on Calvary for all the human race. For He was surely *God's* Lamb, and was slain at the Great, the last real Passover, dear Abraham, if only we all—our race—could see this. What the blood of that first Passover lamb, in Egypt, was in type, to our people in their bondage and Blood-deliverance, so Jesus was in reality."

Moses, of old, wist not how his face shone. And this lovely Jewish maiden, as she talked of her Lord, wist not how all her lovely face was transformed as she talked—*glorified* would not be too strong a description of the change her theme had wrought in her countenance.

"And now, dear Abraham," she went on, "that same Jesus has not only blotted out all my sin, for His name's sake, but he bids me look for Him to come again. When *next* He comes—it may be before even this day closes—"

Cohen shot a quick, puzzled glance at her. She did not notice it but went on:—

"I have learned many things from the scriptures since I have been going to the little Room at Spitalfields, and from the *Word* of Jehovah, Himself, I have learned that Jesus may now come at any moment.

"He will come *in the air*, and will catch away all His believing children. Then, as the teachers show from the *Word* of God, when the church is gone, there shall arise a terrible power, a man who will be Satan's great agent to lead the whole world astray—*Anti*christ, the Word of God calls him—then, during a period, probably about seven years altogether, there shall be an ever growing persecution of those who shall witness boldly for Jesus, and—"

"*Who* will *they* be, Zillah," he interrupted, "if all the

Church,' as you say, will be taken out of the world at the coming of Christ?"

"One of the teachers, the other night, Abraham," she replied, said, "that the natural consequence of the sudden taking away of the Believers from this earth would probably be, at first, a mighty revival, a turning to God. If this be so, then these converts will be the witnesses to Jesus during the awful seven years, which the Word of God calls The Great Tribulation."

"Then too, one of the teachers at the Room said, 'it is possible that not all Christians will be caught up in the air at the coming again of Jesus, but *only* those faithful ones who are found watching, expecting His coming. If that be so—and no one dare dogmatise about so sacred and solemn a thing—then there will be thousands of Christians left behind who will have to pass through the awful time of Antichrist's Tribulation.' "

Her face glowed with holy light, as inspired by the thought in her soul, she went on:—

"At first, dear Abraham, our own race will return to Jerusalem, and to all the land of our Father, still believing in the coming of the Messiah. The temple—that wondrous Temple for which you are working—will be reared to Jehovah. The morning and evening sacrifices will be resumed. Then presently the Antichrist will make our people believe that he is the Messiah. Pretending to be Israel's friend and protector he will deceive them at first, but, by and by, he will try to force idolatory upon them, he will want to set up in our glorious Temple, (which will have been reared to Jehovah,) an idol, an abomination.

"The teacher whom I have heard, Abraham,—and

many of them are of our own race—see from scripture that the great mass of our people, in the land of our fathers, will blindly accept this hideous idol worship.

"But Jehovah will not let Antichrist have all his own way. Jesus, with all those who were caught up with Him into the air, will come to the deliverance of our people. He will come, *this* time, to the earth. He will fight against Antichrist, will overcome him, His feet shall stand on the Mount of Olives.

"Our poor deluded, suffering people will see Him, as our own prophets have said:— *"I will pour out upon the House of David and upon the inhabitants of Jerusalem, the spirit of grace and of supplication,* AND THEY SHALL LOOK UPON ME WHOM THEY HAVE PIERCED, AND THEY SHALL MOURN FOR HIM, *as one mourneth for his only son, and shall be in bitterness for Him, as one that is in bitterness for his first-born."*

She paused abruptly, struck by Cohen's quietude of manner, where she had expected a storm. Gazing up wonderingly into his face she cried:—

"Abraham, why are you thus quiet? Why have you not cursed me for a Meshumed, dear? Can it be that you, too, know aught of these glorious truths?"

There was sadness and kindness in his eyes as he returned her pleading glance. But there was no trace of anger.

"I wonder why, little sister," he began, "I am not angry, as the men of Israel's faith usually are with a Meshumed, even though the defaulter should be as beautiful as Zillah Robart?"

His glance grew kinder, as he went on:—"I began to

wonder where my little sister went, twice a week, in the evenings, and, anxious about her, lest she, in her innocence of heart and ignorance of life, should get into trouble, I followed her one night, and saw that she entered a hall, which I knew to be a preaching-place for Jews."

Zillah's eyes were very wide with wonder. But she did not interrupt him.

"I did not enter the place myself," he went on, "but that very first night, while waiting about for a few minutes, I met an old friend, a Jew like myself, by *race*, but a Christian by faith. He talked with me, pointed to *our* scriptures, quoted from the Gentile New Testament, showed, from them, how, in every detail, the birth, the life, the death of Jesus, the Nazarene, fulfilled the prophecies of our father, and——"

"And you, Abraham—" Zillah laid her hand on the Jew's wrist, in a swift gesture of excitement, "you, dear," she cried, "see that Jesus was the Messiah?"

Slowly, almost sorrowfully it seemed to the eager girl, he shook his head.

"I cannot say all that, Zillah," he went on, "I sat in a seat, last night, in that Hall, where I could see you and Hammond, where I could hear all that was said upon the platform, but where I knew that neither you nor Hammond would be able to see me. All that I heard, last night, dear, has more than half convinced me, but—well, I cannot rush through this matter, I have to remember that it has to do with the life beyond, as well as this life."

He sighed a little wearily.

"I saw the meeting between Hammond and you, Zillah," he went on. "I had before begun to scent something of Hammond's probable feeling for you, and I had seen you look at him in a way that, though you did not yourself probably realize it, meant, I knew, a growing feeling for him warmer than our maidens usually bestow on a Gentile. I saw you enter the cab together, and drive off, and——"

He sighed again. Then without finishing his sentence, he said:

"Perhaps I shall see with you, Zillah, soon. Meanwhile, dear——"

He lifted his hands, let them rest upon her head, and softly, reverently, cried:—

"The Lord bless thee and keep thee; the Lord make his face shine upon thee, and be gracious unto thee; the Lord lift up His countenance upon thee, and give thee peace."

The sweet old Nazarite blessing never fell more tenderly upon human ears than it did upon Zillah Robarts. Jehovah *had* been very gracious to her. She had feared anger, indignation from her brother-in-law, she received blessing instead.

As he slowly lifted his hands from her head, she caught them in hers, lifted them to her lips, and kissed them gratefully.

"May that blessing fall back upon your own head, upon your heart, your life, dear Abraham?" she cried.

Still holding his hands, she lifted her head. An eager light filled all her face, as she added:—

"It wants but a few days to Passover, dear, I shall

pray God that He will reveal Jesus fully to you before that!'

She dropped his hands, and made for the door. "I hear the children from school," she cried. Then she was gone.

Cohen did not turn to his work. But taking a New Testament from his pocket, began to study anew the Passion of Jesus, as recorded in the Gospels.

CHAPTER XX.

THE PLACARD.

RIDING back to his office from that meeting Tom Hammond asked himself:—"Ought I to begin to make this near Return of our Lord for His church, the subject of my 'Prophet's Chamber Column' for to-morrow's issue?"

"I must seek special guidance about this," he presently decided.

The cab was nearing the office when he suddenly murmured:—"HE might come *to-day!*"

Even as he murmured the words his eyes seemed to see a striking way of exhibiting his new-found faith in the Return of his Lord, and he came to a rapid decision.

Lifting the flap in the roof of the cab, he told the driver to go on to a certain Sign and Ticket writer's. Arrived at the place, he explained to the writer that he wanted a card three feet six inches long, proportionate in width, very *boldly,* handsomely written with just the two words upon it, in the order of his sketch.

He had taken an odd piece of card from the man's scrap heap, and with his pencil he drew out his idea, thus:—

TO-DAY?
PERHAPS!

"How soon can I have it?" he asked.

"In a couple of hours, sir!"

"Pack it carefully and I will send a messenger for it!"

Hammond was turning from the counter, when the man said:—

"I beg your pardon, sir, but if it is not too bold a question, may I ask what the two words mean?"

"They mean," smiled Tom Hammond, "that Jesus Christ, God's son, may come suddenly to-day, before even you have time to finish the work upon my order!"

The man's face wore a puzzled look. Then suddenly it brightened a little, as he said:—

"Ah! I sees, its somethink religious. That aint in my line, not a bit, sir. I aint built that way. Now, my misses is! She's the best wife a man ever had, I can't find a speck o' fault wi' her, but, there it is, yer know, she's gone, fair gone, sir, on religious things!"

"Do you love her? Would you like to lose her?" asked Hammond.

"Like to lose her, sir? why, no, sir! I believes I should—I should—well I don't know what I should do, if she wur took!"

There was a note of deep gravity in Tom Hammond's voice, as he said:—

"Then let that motto warn you, as you prepare to write it, that even before you can finish it, the Christ who is to come again, who *will* surely come now very soon, may come. Then, when you go to look for your wife, when you are perhaps expecting her to call you to your tea, she will be missing. You will call her, search for her, yet never find her. Because, if she is a true child of God, she, with all *true* Christians, will have been snatched away unseen from the world, caught up to meet their Lord in the air."

"Good gracious, sir! yer give me the creeps!" gasped the man.

" 'Seek ye the Lord'—your good wife's Lord,—'while He may be found,' my friend." With this parting word Tom Hammond left the shop.

Two hours and a half later the splendid bit of sign writing hung upon the wall of Hammond's room.

It was a most striking placard. The first letter of each word nearly eight inches in length, and in brilliant crimson, the other letters six inches long in deep, purple black.

As he sat back and regarded it where it hung, Tom Hammond mused on all that he had heard that afternoon, of the effects upon the lives of those who possessed a real heart apprehension of the truth of the near Return of the Lord.

"One can scarcely conceive," he murmured, "what London, what all the civilized, and so-called Christian world, would be like, if every man and woman, who *professes* to be a christian, lived in the light of the truth that the Lord's return was near, was imminent. 'Every man' (he was recalling the truth quoted that afternoon, *'Who hath this Hope in him, purifieth himself even as He (Jesus) is pure.'* "

The rest of the day was a busy one. Many callers came in. Everyone noticed the strange placard. Some asked what it meant. Modestly, but with strong purpose, and with perfect frankness, Hammond told each and all who enquired, of his change of heart, and how possessed with the fact that Christ's return was imminent, he had had the placard done for his own, and for others quickening and reminder.

People smiled indulgently, but entered into no argument with him. He was too important a man for that, and equally, they dare not *pooh-pooh* his testimony, wild as it appeared to most, if not all of them.

CHAPTER XXI.

WAS HE MAD?

MADGE, a wife of barely eighteen hours, found her husband's church packed in every nook and corner when she entered it on the Sunday morning.

The news of her sudden return, and equally sudden marriage, had helped to fill the church, though the knowledge that the Rev. Doig was to preach would, in itself, have been sufficient to have gathered an unusually large congregation.

During the pastor's sickness the pulpit had been supplied by various good men, secured by the deacons from all over the county. Doig had preached twice before, and was already a great favourite with the people.

The pastor had not been well enough to be present at any service for many weeks, and as he entered the church this morning, leaning heavily upon his wife's arm, he received quite an ovation from the people.

In spite of the curiosity and excitement over Madge's appearance, the congregation speedily settled down to quiet worship. There was something subducing, quieting in the preacher's manner. Just before the address, the people sang :—

> "Lo! God is here! let us adore,
>   And own how dreadful is this place!
> Let all within us feel His power,
>   And silent bow before His face;
> Who know His power, His grace who prove,
> Serve Him with awe, with reverence, love."

With the singing of this hymn a deep, deep solemnity

came down upon the assembly. It deepened as the preacher unfolded the wonders of the Bible revelation relating to the Lord's second coming.

Madge forgot her husband, as, absorbed by the wonder of the revelation, she drank in the glorious truth. Had she been more alert in watching the pastor, she would have seen how restless he grew! How angrily his eyes flashed! How scowling his beetling brows became.

Some of the people noticed their pastor's evident displeasure, and so did one or two of the deacons. But no one dreamed that he would dare to utter any dissent to the service.

Was he mad? Perhaps he was, for the time, as many men and women become, who nurse a groundless, senseless anger and jealousy! He was jealous of this man's hold upon the people. He had not dreamed that any man could hold his congregation, as this man was holding them. He was angry, too, at the doctrine preached.

With a startling suddenness he leaped to his feet, forgetting his weakness, as he cried:—

"I will not have that lying, senseless nonsense—worse than nonsense—preached in *my* church, Mr. Doig. You will either announce another text, and take a different subject, sir, or you must cease to preach!"

A slight flush rose into the cheeks of the preacher, as he half turned to the pastor, and in low, but firm voice, heard everywhere amid the sudden strained silence, he said:—

"Dear Pastor, if you insist, (you have the *legal* right to do so, as *pastor* of this church, I suppose) I will desist. But I cannot, if I preach on, do other than declare all that God would have me do. Why, even as we are here, our Loving Lord may come, and if I faltered in my testimony I should have to meet Him ashamedly —and—"

"Rot!" muttered the pastor. The word was heard by everyone, and a murmur of strong dissent ran through the place.

With a white angry face, and flashing savage eyes, the Pastor walked to the table, and leant upon it heavily in his weakness, as he cried hoarsely, "This service is now concluded. While I hold the pastorate, no such sentimental rubbish, as Mr. Doig seems bent upon giving us, shall be voiced from this platform."

One of the deacons protested. The pastor was firm. Passion had rendered him temporarily irresponsible. Another of the deacons, who had been conferring with Doig—who had whispered the facts of the pastor's evident temporary irresponsibility—now urged the people to disperse quietly.

Doig walked down to his host, and whispered, "if I go at once, it will help matters." The pair then left the church. The congregation followed quickly. The deacons remained behind to confer together over the situation, which was of a hitherto unheard of character.

*   *   *   *   *   *   *

The pastor had left by the side door, and leaning more heavily than ever upon Madge, they made their way to the house of Thaddeus Finisterre, Madge's father. They were staying there. They took a private way, by which they were spared the unpleasantness of meeting any of the congregation.

Four minutes took them to the house. Neither of them spoke during the brief journey. For the first time

in her life Madge knew what it was to feel the touch
of fear. She had married the man by her side knowing
comparatively little of his real character and tempera-
ment.

"There may be insanity in his family," she mused, as
she walked by his side. She had already told herself
that nothing but a temporary touch of madness could
have led to his outburst in the church.

Arrived at the house, the pastor went straight to his
room, this gave Madge an opportunity to confer with her
father and mother a moment.

"His long anxious illness has unsettled his brain a
little!" the mother said. "The best thing will be to take
no notice, let us all be as cheerful, as much like our
ordinary selves, as we can. Then, if we can persuade
him to go away to-morrow, I guess the best thing for you
to do, Madge, will be to get a good doctor to examine
him, and to prescribe for him."

The dinner-meal which followed, presently, was fairly
free of constraint. After dinner Mr. and Mrs. Finisterre
slipped away and left the husband and wife to themselves.

Almost immediately the pair were left, the pastor began
to abuse the preacher of the morning, and to denounce
the teaching of the Lord's second coming.

"But, my dear," cried Madge, "it is evidently almost
the most prominent doctrine in the New Testament.
There are more direct references to it in the New Testament, Mr. Doig said, than to any other revealed doctrine."

"But its not *my* doctrine," snapped the pastor, "not
the doctrine of *our* church. It was scoffed at at our col-
lege, when *I* was a student, and—and—"

Madge gazed wonderingly at him. His argument seemed so puerile, if not actually sinful.

"But," she cried, "I don't see how that argument holds. To me, it sounds like blasphemy, almost, to say I, as a *minister,* and *we* as a *church,* will not preach the most prominent doctrine of the New Testament, because of the foolish abuse of the teaching by here and there a wild visionary who lets his fancy and whim run away with his judgment. Suppose, dear Homer, some church or minister should say, 'We wont preach the doctrine of the Atonement,' would that save them from the charge of blasphemy, when God says:

" 'If any man shall take away from the words of the book of this prophecy, God shall take away his part out of the Book of Life, and out of the Holy City, and from the things which are written in his Book.' "

The pastor gazed at her in amazement. Her fashion of putting the matter gave him small opportunity of replying, so he took refuge in the coarse sneer:—

"Have you turned *Doigite?*"

With a quick flush in her cheeks, and sudden flashing of eye, Madge replied:—

"If by that you mean, do I see, and have I accepted the revelation of the Word of God, as to the near coming of Christ, then I say '*yes.*' I am *not* a Doigite, but I am, thank God, a Christian! A very young one, a very poor and inexperienced one, 'tis true, but still I am one, and am desirous to live to the Lord to whom I have given myself, and, after all I heard from the preacher this morning, I am more than ever determined to serve Christ wholly, and I can quite see how this wondrous *fact* of the near Return of our Lord will be a new and mighty force to revolutionize all my life."

An ugly snarl curled the lips of the amazed, discom-fited pastor, and he was just beginning a cruel little speech, when one of the Deacons was announced.

Madge left the two men alone. As she passed on to her own room there was a terrible pain at her heart, for the hideous thought came to her:—"Can Homer be truly converted? If he is, how can it be that he flatly refuses to believe what God has so plainly revealed?"

CHAPTER XXII.

FROM THE PROPHET'S CHAMBER.

TOM HAMMOND was alone in his editorial office. He had come to the day, the moment at last, when he felt constrained to write out of his full heart, to the readers of his paper, all that he yearned that the world should know of the imminence of the Return of the Lord.

Before he put pen to paper to write on this supreme theme in his "Prophet's Chamber" column, he bowed his head on his desk and prayed for guidance and help. Then he began to write out his heart fully, telling first of his conversion, and of the wondrous meetings conducted by Major H——.

His whole being was fired with holy purpose. "Had ever a preacher such a pulpit as has the editor of "The Courier?" he wrote. "Had any preacher ever so mighty a privilege, so great a responsibility as is mine to-day? This paper circulates through more than a million people's hands, even allowing that only the one person purchasing the paper, reads it—though one might almost safely double that million, since there are very few of the papers which will not be read by *two*, or more persons.

"This 'Prophet's Column' will likely overflow all its ordinary banks, as does the Great Nile in its season, but if my overflowing but carry life on its tide, as does the tide of the overflowing Nile, then, all will be well.

"As a converted Editor of a great daily, I have put my hand, my pen, my mind into the mighty, unerring hand of God, praying that I may write only that whicn will reach the *hearts* of my readers. And the question comes to me, 'what word does London, does England most need to-day?'

"This—that all the world should know, and realize, that any day, aye, any hour, Christ may return—not to the earth but *into the air*—"

Here followed the teaching of the Gospel and Epistles, as he had learned it from Major H——, and from his own subsequent personal study of the Word of God.

"I appeal to the most thoughtful of my readers, I appeal to the unthinking, as I say, 'do you not see how a real belief, in this near coming of Christ would revolutionize all our national, commercial, domestic, and church life. How, too, it would immediately settle everv social problem.'

"If our legislators, sitting in council at St. Stephens, realized that before the present Parliamentary session could end in the ordinary way, that Christ might come, what a speedy end they would seek to put to every national iniquity.

"The hideous drink traffic would be swept, root and branch, from our land. And, in sweeping that curse away, the awful problem of the unemployed, the homeless, the starving, all that inures to our national poverty would be swept away.

"The shameful opium traffic with China; the national Greed for territory; the Traffic in White Slaves; and every other national iniquity would be abolished

"Christian churches, (so-called) would become worthy of the name *Christian*. All those bits of devilish device used to extract, and extort money from the pockets of the people would end, as by magic. Theatricals would be left to the theatres; nigger entertainments would be left to the music-halls; the church would leave all these things to their master—*the Devil.*

"In *social* life, people would pay their debts; the wild, mad, sinful extravagance that marks the life of to-day, would cease. Christians would love one another. Every Evangelical denomination would be *inter*-denominational in the truest sense, and be *one* wholly in their Crucified, Risen, coming Lord. A love for the poor fallen world, such as has never been since our Lord spent Himself in service, would be the order of the day, and not the vision of a few. Every missionary society would have more men and women and money than they actually needed.

"But, even as I pen this millenium-like picture, I know, from the Word of God, that it *cannot* be *before* Christ comes. But I seek to arouse every *Christian* to God's call to them on this matter. You, who profess to be Christ's, dare not refuse this truth, save at the peril of losing the *Crown* of Life.

"The vast bulk of the churches, I know, preach, that the world will continually improve until the earth shall be fit for Christ to come and reign. But I defy any cleric or layman to show me a single word of scripture that gives the faintest colour to that belief, or statement —unless the person wrests the passage so advanced from its distinctly marked *dispensational* setting.

"Things (spiritual) are growing worse and worse. There is a wholesale down-gradeism, too awful to con-template. 'Priest and people have erred alike!' I take up the official organ of a section of the church that has ever been regarded as the most out-an-out, in all that pertains to Evangelical truth, and I find its great head saying 'The Bible is *not* the sole spiritual guide for the christian, for, practically, the Bible is a *dead* book!'

"The chief leader-writer of that same paper—himself usually regarded as the soundest of Believers, the most trenchent of all Evangelical preachers, writes in one of a series of articles, 'That the so-called *Finished work* of Christ, is a doctrine not to be found in scripture,' and glories in the fact that *'we* never have, and, I trust, we never shall, preach this doctrine.'

"All this but proves the truth of the New Testament prophecies, '*Perilous* times shall come,' 'Evil men and seducers shall wax worse and worse, *deceiving,* and *being deceived.'* If only we could all be induced to read the signs of the times in the light of scripture! we should then realize that we were in the thickest darkness of the world's blackest night, the darkness immediately pre-ceeding the dawn, and we should be looking for 'the Morning Star.' "

Here, writing with swift, eager pen, he went over the ground covered by Major H——, as regarded the signs of the coming of the Lord—the movement among the Jews; their excitement, as a race, over the date discovery 5,666; the preparations for the re-building of the Temple. Then the increased effort in the Foreign Mission fields. The growth of the spirit of lawlessness in the world, and in the church. The multiplicity of spiritualistic devices—*doctrine of Devils*. The awaken-ing of all real, true, spiritually-minded Bible *students* to the fact of Christ's near Return. And the great, but often disregarded sign, "the scoffers who shall say where is the promise of His coming? for, since the Fathers fell asleep, all things continue as they were from the beginning of creation."

"But He *will* come! He is near at hand! Every sign of the times proclaims this! It is NIGHT, now, and He will come as a thief in the night. At any moment now we may look for Him. Before this news-sheet, damp from the press, is in the hands of my readers, Christ *may* have come and taken away *every one* of His own Believing people—*I* shall be missing, another here, and another there will be missing.

"And when a puzzled, troubled London shall be gathering in business, that saying shall have come to pass, *'The one shall be taken, the other left!'* (For though this word is *primarily Jewish* in its application, it will yet have a measure of meaning for the world, when the Church is taken away).

"May every *Christian* be ready to meet His Lord, when He shall come, and every unready, unsaved soul who reads these 'Prophet's Chamber' columns, seek the face of God through faith in the Atoning work of Jesus Christ. For, believe me, His Return is very near, to some of us the sound of His footfalls is even now in our ears."

He bent his head over the written sheets, praying God to bless the message. Then an interruption came. A knock at the door, and his sub, Ralph Bastin entered.

CHAPTER XXIII.

PASSOVER!

COHEN, the Jew, blew out the candle, and set the stand aside. The knees of his trousers were pressed and dusty. He had just been over the whole house, lighted candle in hand, and had searched every nook and crannie, every cupboard, every shelf, under the edge of every carpet, looking for the faintest sign of leaven in the form of bread, cake, or biscuit crumb. He had found nothing, and went to his room to bathe and change his clothing.

"What of you, Zillah?" he had asked the lovely girl, earlier in the day. "With your newly-espoused faith in the Nazarene, shall you partake of the lamb with us?"

"Certainly, I will," she replied, "*only* I shall take the meal more in the spirit of the Lord's Supper, of the Christian Church. And Abraham——"

Her eyes, as they were lifted to his, swam with tender, pitying tears, as she added:

"All the time I shall be praying that you may meet the Christ of God, Jesus of Nazareth; and while you seek to remember our people's deliverance from the land of Bondage, I shall be praying that you, dear Abram, may be delivered from the bondage of the legalism of our ra

* * * * * * *

The Passover table was spread in Cohen's house. The arrangement of that table was a curious mixture of Mosaic and Rabbinical command. In the case of all but

really very pious Jews of this day, the real and actual
Passover is not kept.

Passover—(*chag Appesach* of the Jews) *must* have
a lamb roasted to make it the *real* feast, the ordinary
Jew to-day, contents himself with an egg, and a burnt
shank-bone of mutton, and unleavened cakes.

Cohen's Passover Feast always included a small lamb.
Still, Rabbinical lore and Bible command were curiously
mixed in the Cohen celebration.

The table, to-night, had an egg according to Rabbinical
order, but there was a tiny roast lamb as well. There
was the glass dish of bitter herbs; the salt water, typify-
ing the tears of Israelitish misery in Egypt; a dish of
almonds, apples, and other fruit, chopped and mixed,
represented the lime and mortar of the Brick-making in
the Land of Bondage.

Chervil and parsley were there, and lettuce. A large
pile of unleavened cakes, a big coloured glass ewer with
unfermented wine and water, and many other items
considered to be the orthodox thing at the Feast.

All the Cohen household was there. Zillah, radiant
with the glow of the new life in Christ that had come to
her.

Rachel, her sister, was red-eyed and sullen. Zillah
had been pleading with her to open her mind, and her
heart to the Christian teaching of the Messiah who had
come, and who had atoned for *all* the race, Jew and
Gentile alike.

Angry and sullen, the wife had said hard things of
Zillah. Her frivolous, irresponsible nature was more
than satisfied with the barest *form* of the faith of her
race.

The two children were full of suppressed excitement, the elder—the boy—especially.

Cohen, the head of the house, was singularly quiet and grave. His eyes had a far-away look in them. He looked like a man moving in a trance.

Presently the boy, (he had been carefully coached) asked, according to the usual formula:

"What mean ye, father, by this Service?"

Cohen's eyes stared over the head of his son, and in a voice very unlike its usual tones, replied:—

"It is the Sacrifice of Jehovah's Passover, who halted by the blood-sprinkled houses of our fathers in Egypt, that the destroying angel should come not nigh, when He smote the Egyptians, but preserved our fathers."

"Will our people *ever* do this, father?" queried the boy.

"Till Messiah come, they will, dear son?" The strained gaze of Cohen, as he answered, was as though he was trying to pierce Time's veil, and see the coming Messiah approaching.

"When will Messiah come, father?" continued the boy.

"To-night, perhaps, my son. Set His chair! Open the door!"

Swiftly, but with remarkable quietude, for a child, the boy placed a chair at the table, then, stepping briskly, silently to the door, he set it wide open, and left it thus, and returned to his place by the table.

Rachel took the ewer and poured out a little wine and water into each glass. In her sullenness, as she came to Zillah's glass, she slopped the wine over the edge. The children glanced curiously from the spilled wine to the face of their aunt, then at their father's face.

Zillah's face flushed; Cohen's grew pale, and set in a

sharp spasm of pain. No word was said, each took up their glass, and drank the *first* cup of blessing.

There was a moment's pause, then Cohen spread his hands, bowed his head, and repeated "The Blessing:—"

"The Lord bless us and keep us; the Lord make His face shine upon us and be gracious unto us. The Lord lift up the light of his countenance upon us and give us peace."

Under her breath, yet distinctly heard by Cohen, in the solemn hush that followed the Blessing, Zillah murmured:—

"But now, in Christ Jesus, ye who sometimes were afar off, are made nigh by the blood of Christ. FOR HE IS OUR PEACE."

Cohen glanced quietly at her. She met the glance with one of intense yearning. He translated it rightly, as meaning "If *only* you could see this truth?"

There were two bowls of water set on a side-board. Cohen and his wife rinsed their hands in one bowl, Zillah and the two children in the other.

Addressing himself to his son, more than to the others, Cohen, when they had returned to the table, as the head of the house was instructed to do, explained why they *sat* at the Feast:—

"Our Fathers, when they took the Feast for the *first* time in Egypt, my son, took it *standing,* with their loins girt, and their staff in hand, for *they* were starting on that great journey that eventually lasted forty years. But we, their descendents, eat the feast to-day, *sitting* at our ease, as a symbol that our people have been delivered from the cruel bondage."

Then the *first* Hallel was repeated.—Psalms 113, and 114. The *second* cup of Blessing was taken by each.

Then Cohen asked a Blessing on *each* kind of food on the table. Then he carved a portion of lamb for each one, they took their seats, and the meal began.

The children were excused from eating the stinging bitter herbs. But Cohen, Rachel, and Zillah, each took a little with their lamb and unleavened bread.

Conversation became fairly general over the meal, except that Rachel's sullen anger increased, and she kept silent.

At the conclusion of the meal, the *third* cup of Blessing was drunk, and Cohen repeated the 115, 116, 117, 118, Psalm. At the close of the Hallel, the *fourth*, and last cup of Blessing was taken. The Feast was over.

A sudden silence fell upon them all. No one moved, no one spoke, for a moment. Suddenly Zillah broke the dead silence. She had a glorious voice, and she let it ring out in that wondrous song:—

> "Not all the blood of beasts
>   On Jewish altars slain
> Could give the guilty conscience peace,
>   Or wash away our stain."

No one interrupted. Cohen *could* not, for the thrall of some strange, new power was upon him. His wife was furious—but kept her fury bottled up The children were delighted, they loved to hear their aunt sing, and to the amaze of their father and mother—they joined in the singing, for, with other children, they had often of late been to the evening meeting for Jewish children. And Zillah, who had talked with them, believed that they loved the Christ.

Without a break, the three voices sang on:

> "But Christ the Heavenly Lamb,
>   Takes all our sins away;
> A sacrifice of nobler name,
>   And richer Blood than they.

> "My faith would lay her hand
>   On that meek head of Thine,
> While as a penitent I stand,
>   And here confess my sin.
>
> "My soul looks back to see
>   The burden Thou didst bear
> When hanging on the accursed tree,
>   And knows her guilt was there.
>
> "Believing we rejoice
>   To feel the curse remove;
> We bless the Lamb with cheerful voice,
>   And trust His bleeding love."

Again, for full thirty seconds, as the glorious song finished, there was an absolute silence, save for the ricketting of Rachel's chair, as she moved in pettish anger on her seat.

Zillah had kept her eyes fixed upon Cohen's face all the time she was singing, and had seen a strangely wondrous light slowly gather in his eyes. She had known, for days, that he was very, very near to the point of acceptance of Christ. Even as they had gathered at the table of the Passover, she was not sure, but that in all but profession and testimony, he was a Christian.

Now he suddenly broke the silence.

"Sing the last two verses again, Zillah" he said.

> "*My* soul looks back to see
>   The burden Thou didst bear
> When hanging on the accursed tree,
>   And knows her guilt was there.

Zillah's glorious voice rang out. And now, even to *her* wonder, Cohen's deeper tones joined hers. Her heart leaped as she noted the emphasis he put upon the "*My* soul."

She sang on. His voice sang on too. Then came

the last verse, and in a perfect burst of triumph, his voice rang out:—

> "Believing *I* rejoice
> To feel the curse remove;
> *I* bless the Lamb with cheerful voice,
> And trust His bleeding love!"

It was a strangely ecstatic moment for Zillah. Tears flooded her eyes, she tried to speak, but her emotion choked her.

Cohen stood up. His face was ablaze with the wonder of the revelation that had come to him. He spread his hands upward, and his eyes were lifted in the same direction, as he cried:—

"Thou loving Christ! Thou Precious Jesus! I am *Thine*—THINE—THINE—!"

Then he remembered his wife.

"Machael, wife of my heart. Jesus is the Messiah!"

"Rachael, dear heart," he cried, as he moved to her side.

"Bah!" she cried. With a thrust of her hand and foot, she kept him from her. Then in tones of withering scorn and disgust, she cried:

"Mehusmed!"

He bent over her very tenderly, stooping to meet her eyes, and trying to take her hand.

The two children clung to Zillah, and the boy suddenly began to pipe out, in his clear treble, the hymn so beloved of Jewish children who attend the mission meetings.

> "Come to the Saviour, Make no delay,"

Rachael shot a fiercely angry glance in the boy's direction, then without looking at her husband, she thrust at him, to prevent his taking her hand, as she cried:—

"Accursed! Mehusmed! Don't touch *me!*"

"But, Rachael!" he began tenderly.

She flung herself sharply round upon him and spat full in his face. Then she turned sharply from him again.

A full half minute went by. The room grew so eerily still that it startled her. She turned to gaze where the quartette had been.

The room was empty save for herself!

With a cry she started to her feet. They could not have gone out of the door for her chair had all the time stood right in the way. What was this then that had happened?

Her breath came hot and laboured. Her eye-balls bulged horribly! A reeling sickness began to steal over her. She dropped back, terrified, in her chair, gasping:—

"Zillah said this morning "The Christ will come *soon, suddenly,* then those who are His, will be taken, unseen, unheard, from the world!"

With a sharp, anguished cry, he let her bulging, terror-filled eyes sweep the room again as she cried:—

"And my *children,* too!"

Her eyes were tearless, but dry, hard sobs shook all her frame.

The next moment a kind of frenzy seized her. She rushed to the front door, and into the street. She would find out if any one else was missing.

A little crowd was on the pavement. A hansom cab stood by the curb. The fare was standing on the front board. He was a minister of some kind. He wore a M.B. waistcoat, a clerical collar, a soft, wide-brimmed, black felt hat. He glanced up at the driver's seat, as he cried:—

"But *some* one, *surely*, must have seen what became of him. If he fell off his box in a fit, where is his body?"

"I seed him one hinstant," cried a voice from the crowd, "I wur lookin straight at 'im, 'cos I sed to myself, taint often as yer see a kebby wear a white 'at, now-a-days. Then, while I wur starin' at 'im, he sort o' disappeared, the reins fell on the roof o' the keb, the 'oss stopped, an—"

"He's gone!" shrieked a woman's voice.

It was Rachael. Bare-headed, dressed in all her festal finery, she had just rushed down the steps of the house, and heard the question and answer as to the disappearance of the hansom driver. The crowd turned and faced her, her shrill tones had startled them.

"He's gone to Jehovah!" she screamed again. "My husband, my sister, my two children—we were at Passover—we——"

With a piercing shriek she flung up her arms, laughed hideously and fell in a huddled heap on the bottom step of the flight.

CHAPTER XXIV.

"THIS SAYING SHALL COME TO PASS."

TOM HAMMOND greeted his *sub* most heartily. Ralph had been away, in Paris, for a fortnight, partly on business, partly for a change.

As soon as their greetings were exchanged, he turned eagerly to Hammond, as he said:—

"But I say, old man, what on earth is all this jargon you wrote me about, the return of the Christ, and——"

He paused suddenly. His eyes had just caught sight of the great placard. His gaze was riveted on it. He read the two words aloud:—

"TODAY? PERHAPS!"

In a voice of wondering amaze, he gasped:—

"What's *that*, Tom? What *does* it mean?"

Tom Hammond repeated, in a few sentences, what he had previously written to his friend, as to his conversion, then, passing on to the subject of the Lord's second coming, he said:

"I am so impressed, Ralph, with the imminence of our Lord's return, that I have had that placard done to arrest the attention of callers upon me, and give me an opportunity of speaking to them about their eternal destiny. To-day, too, I have been impressed so with the necessity of speaking to the world—"The Courier's" world, I mean of course—on this great, this momentus subject, that I have made it the subject of my 'Prophet's Chamber' column."

He gathered up the sheets of his M.S. he had written,

and passed them over the table to Ralph Bastin.

"You will see, I have written it in the most simple, almost colloqual style, Ralph," he said. "I wanted it to be a man's quiet, earnest, simple utterance to his fellow man, and not a journalist's article."

Ralph Bastin's eyes raced over the papers. His face was a strange study, while he read, reflecting a score of different, ever-changing emotions, but amid them all never losing a constant deepening amaze.

As he finished the last sheet, he looked Tom Hammond hard and searchingly in the face.

"My dear Tom," he began. His voice was very grave, very serious. "You'll ruin The Courier! You will ruin yourself! The world will call you mad——!"

"They called my Lord mad, Ralph, and they have called His servants mad, over and over again, ever since."

There was not a shadow of cant in his voice and manner, as he went on:—

"The word of our God, Ralph—which is the *only real* rule of life, tells us that Christ, whose name I profess, said:—

" 'Whosoever shall confess me, before men, him will I confess also before my Father which is in Heaven. . . . If any man will come after Me, *let him deny himself,* and take up his cross *daily,* and follow Me. For whosoever will save his life shall lose it: but whosoever will lose his life, for My sake, the same shall save it. For what is a man advantaged, if he gain the whole world and lose his own soul. . . .

" 'For whosoever shall be ashamed of me *and of My words.*' ('*Surely I come quickly,*' Ralph, is one of *His very last* recorded words,) 'of him shall the Son of Man

be ashamed, when He shall come in His own glory, and
in His Father's, and of the holy angels.' "

Tom Hammond leant forward in his chair to lay his
hand on the wrist of the other, to plead with him. But,
with an exclamation of angry impatience, Ralph, cried:

"Hang it, old man, you must be going dotty!"

With an expression of annoyance, almost amounting
to disgust, he swung round on his heel.

"Look here, Tom," he began.

He swirled back to meet his friend face to face.

Then, with a startled cry, he stared at the chair, in
which, an instant before, Tom Hammond had been sitting.

The chair was empty!

"Good God!" he gasped.

Instinctively he knew what had happened! Involuntarily his eyes travelled to the Placard, and in the same
moment he recalled the closing words of Tom Hammond's M.S. which he had just read:—

" '*Then shall it come to pass, that which is written,*
"ONE SHALL BE TAKEN, THE OTHER LEFT.' "

A strange, unnatural trembling seized him. He dropped into the chair he had been occupying, and stared
at the empty revolving chair opposite.

"Good——God!" He slowly repeated the words.
There was no thought of irreverence in the utterance.
It was the unconscious acknowledgment of God's Pres-
ence and Power.

For a time—he never knew how long—he sat still
and silent like a man stunned. Then, as his eyes travelled
slowly to where the sheets of M.S.'s lay, he smiled wearily, drew them towards him, and took his stylo from his
pocket. Putting the most powerful pressure of his will

upon himself, he began to write after the last works penned by his translated chief:—

(P.S.—Written by the sub-editor of "The Courier." By the time this printed sheet is being read, the world will have learned that a section of the community has been suddenly taken from our midst. The Editor of The Courier, the giant mind and kindly heart of Tom Hammond, have been taken from us.

The writer of this postscript, who was in the room, when the "Prophet" of The Courier was taken, was in the act of scorning his message as to the nearing of the great translation. "In a moment, in the twinkling of an eye" he was gone.

The writer has not left the room since, and has no means of knowing who else among those known to him are missing,—not many *personal* acquaintances, he fears, since one's personal clique has never shown any very marked signs of what one has *hitherto* considered an *ultra* type of Christianity, a condition of *"righteous overmuch."*

"When we pass out of this room, presently, and touch the great outside world once more, what shall we find? How soon will it be generally known that a section of the community—a larger section, maybe, than we conceive possible—has been silently, suddenly, secretly taken from our midst? What will follow? Where are the prophets who shall teach us where we are, and what we may expect? Does the end of the world follow next? Is there any order of events, specified in the Bible, that follows this mysterious translatior if so, what is it? Who will show us these things?

"Again, since I, the writer of this postscript, am left, while my friend, Hammond, is taken, *why am I left,* and why shall I find—as of course I shall when I begin to go abroad among mine acquaintance—hundreds of others *left?* I have been christened, confirmed, have occasionally 'communicated,'—this is the clerical term, though as I write, it occurs to me that there must have been some flaw, somewhere, in the '*communicating.*'

"I have always supposed myself a Christian by virtue of these things, to which a clean, decent life has been added. Thousands upon thousands, I feel sure, will be puzzled by this same contemplation, when this wonderful Translation becomes generally known.

"If we are not made Christians by christening, confirmation, communicating, why have we always been taught so, by our clergy? How many of these same clergy shall we find *left* behind.

"And I suppose there will have been some kind of kindred process at work among the Nonconformists bodies—in pulpit and pew, alike. For ourselves, we have come little in contact with Nonconformity, but, if what is accepted generally, to-day, as to the religious situation, be true—that the curse of the Ritualism of the 'Establishment,' finds its parralel in the Rationalism, Unitarianism, Socialism, etc., of Nonconformity—then I shall expect to find as many Nonconformists, lay and ministerial, *left* behind from this mysterious, spiritual translation, as churchmen."

There came a tap at the door. The messenger boy Charley, appeared. He glanced towards the empty Editor's chair, then stammered.

"I beg pardon, sir, I thought Mr. Hammond was here, sir. They have jest blown up the tube to know if the 'Prophet's' column was ready."

Ralph Bastin noticed that the eyes of the boy flitted from his face to the placard.

"Know what that means, Charley?" Bastin asked.

"Yus, sir, leastways, I knows what Mr. Hammond means by it! E sez that Jesus Christ's comin' back, an' goin' to take all the real Christians out 'er the world, an' nobody wont see 'em go, nor nothink. I 'eard Mr. Hammond 'splainin' it all to a gent, t'other day."

Curious to know if the boy himself had thought seriously at all of the matter, Bastin said:—

"What do *you* think of it, Charley?"

"Wal, it's like this, sir, I aint been to no Sunday School since I wus quite a young 'un, 'bout eight perhaps. An' I never goes to no Church nor Chapel, cos why? Why 'cos Sunday's the only day—'cepts my 'olidays—when I gits any chance fur any rickreation or fresh hair. So I aint up much in 'ligious things. But my sister, Lulu, she walks out wi' a chap as teaches in a Sunday School—leastways, he oosed to afore he took up wi' our Lulu, but now 'e wants 'is Sunday School time fur spoonying, an' 'e can spoon, sir, there's no error—well, knowin' as 'e oosed to do summat at 'ligion, I ups an' arsks 'im about what Mr. Hammond said, about that takin' away business, an 'e (Jimmy Doubleyou, Lulu's chap, I mean, sir,) larfed, an' said, "Don't yer b'lieve any sich rot! D'yer think Gawd 'ud go an' *kidnap* all 'Is people like that?"*

Ralph Bastin would have smiled, at any other time,

<hr>

* At a Bible-Reading in Malvern in the house of one of God's choicest saints, Miss Ann Boobbyer, where the precious truth of *"The Rapture"* was being unfolded, a minister present, who was much used of God, as an evangelist, started up, and cried,

"What! My Lord coming to *Kidnap* all His people? Never! Never! I'll not believe that!"

at this curious reply. But, to-night, his soul was too
sobered. Gathering up the sheets of M.S.'s, he clipped
them together, stamped them with Hammond's mechan-
ical imprimatur, and handed the sheaf to the lad, giving
him instructions to deliver them in the Composing Room.

As the lad left the room, he sat back in his chair,
and tried to think out the position of affairs. He had
hardly settled himself down, before the messenger boy
returned.

" 'Scuse me, sir," the lad began, "but summat curious
hev 'appened. There's two 'holy Joes,' in the Composing room, an' one in the Sterio room—leastways, they
oosed to be—an' they's all three bunked off, somewheres,
nobody seed 'em go, an their coats an' 'hats is 'ung hup
where they ussally is, an' some o' the chaps says as they's
translated. Alf Charman, one o' the comp's, oosed to
talk like Mr. 'Ammond did, sir——"

The boy looked a trifle fearsomely at the empty editor's chair, as he added.

"Mr. 'Ammond, sir, I—er—I suppose as—'e—'e aint
——."

"Mr. Hammond has gone out!" Bastin rapped out the
words quite sharply. All this talk of the missing men
was getting on his nerves.

"That will do, Charley!" he added.

The lad walked slowly to the door, his eyes fixed on
the placard, his lips moving to the words, *"To-day?"*
"Perhaps!"

"Coorius!" he muttered as he passed out of the room.

Ralph Bastin tried again to settle himself down for
a quiet think. Suddenly he started to his feet, wild
of eye, and with horror in his face.

"Viola?" he muttered. "My beautiful little Viola?

She has talked continuously of the Christ of late. Has she been——?"

He seized his hat, and with a crushed down sob of literal fear, he rushed away.

Outside the office he came upon a hanson. He leaped into it, shouting the Bloomsbury address to the man.

"Drive for your life!" he yelled. "A sovereign for you if you get me there quickly!"

The man's horse was fresh. They rushed through the streets. Arriving at the house, he tossed the driver his promised sovereign, and letting himself in with his latch key, he dashed into the drawing room. It was empty!

He was leaving the room hurriedly, when he encountered the landlady. "Miss Viola has gone to bed, sir, she overtired herself, visiting the sick-poor with her flowers, and all that, to-day, and she——"

"Thanks!" with a hurried nod he raced up the stairs. The child's bedroom was next to his own. He entered it without knocking. He was too much agitated to stand upon ceremony.

The room was in darkness, he struck a match, laid it to the gas nipple, then shot a quick glance at the bed. In that first glance, he saw that it was empty. He went close up to the bed, it had been occupied, he could see that. He thrust his hand well down under the clothes. There was faint body warmth left in the bedding—or it seemed so to him.

"God help me?" he groaned. And two great tears fell glittering from his eyes.

"Viola! Viola! my precious darling!" he moaned. "You were my life, my——"

His emotion choked him. He was dropping into the chair by the bed-side, when he noticed that the back and seat of the chair were strewn with the under-clothing, which the child had evidently placed there when disrobing.

With eyes blinded with tears, he lifted the dainty garments in a pile, and laid them on the foot of the bed. Then he dropped back into the chair, buried his face in the pillow—the impress of the lost, beautiful head was left in the pillow—and wept.

For five minutes he remained thus. Then rousing himself, he muttered:—"I must play the man! and get back to the office and lay hold of things."

He left the room, and managed to clear the house without encountering his landlady. Lucky in finding a hansom, he had himself driven first to the central News Agency. He wanted to find out if anything of the mystery was generally known.

The careless-minded, light-hearted tapists, clerks and journalists, were laughing over the few vague rumours of the translation that had reached them.

He said nothing of what he knew, and drove on to the office.

"If the world has to go on, for a time, just as it *has* been going, in spite of this wonderful thing," he muttered, "then, as acting editor of the Courier, I had better stifle every feeling, save the professional, and give London—England—the best morning issue under the new condition of things."

CHAPTER XXV.

FOILED!

THIN and pale, but with the likeness of God shining in her dark eyes—there was the bruise-like colour of great exhaustion under each eye—Mrs. Joyce sat wearily stitching at her warehouse needle-work.

Jem Joyce, the drunken, reprobate husband, was serving a six weeks sentence for his old crime, drunken disorderliness in the streets, and assaulting the police. His time would soon be up. The fearsome wife had recalled the fact, that very day, though she could not be sure of the *actual* date.

As she worked now her voice whispered low in song:—

> "It may be in the evening,
>   When the work of the day is done,
> And you have time to sit in the twilight
>   And watch the sinking sun,
> When the long, bright day dies slowly
>   Over the sea,
> And the hour grows quiet and holy
>   With thoughts of Me;
> While you hear the village children
>   Passing along the street,
> Among those thronging footsteps
>   May come the sound of *My* feet.
> Therefore I tell *you*: Watch
>   By the light of the evening-star,
> When the room is growing dusky
>   As the clouds afar;
> Let the door be on the latch
>   In your home,
> For it may be through the gleaming
>   I will come."

Low, soft, yearning in its passionate longing for her

Lord's Return, she began again to hum her lay, when a step sounded somewhere near. So keenly had her imagination been aroused by her song, and by her long, yearning-dwelling on the theme of the song, that she, almost unconsciously to herself, rose to her feet, her work and needle held lightly in her hand, her face turned towards the door. For one instant, her imagination had suggested the step to have been her Lord's.

The next moment she turned deadly pale. She had recognized the step. It was her husband's.

She had just time to drop back into her chair, and, tremblingly, to resume her work, when the brute entered. He was drunk—viciously, murderously drunk.

He began to curse her, the moment he crossed the threshold. He called her foul names that brought the flush of a great shame—for *him*, not for herself—to her cheeks. He sneered at her religion, and blasphemed the name of her Lord.

Her lips moved, but no sound came from them. She prayed for grace to be silent, for she feared to aggravate him. Suddenly, he shook his fist in her face, and hissed:—

"Curse you! You ——! Do you know I've only come back to you to settle all my scores. I've come to——"

His foaming, blaspheming rage choked him, and he leaped forward, (she had drawn back from his clenched fist) and caught her by the throat.

She could not cry out. She thought his purpose was to strangle her. He glared murderously back into her eyes, which his awful grip was forcing from their sockets. He shook her fiercely, hurling hideous blasphemies at her all the time. Then he essayed to put his real purpose in view, and drawing himself up, and drawing her, at the same time, towards himself, he hurled himself forward to dash her head against the wall of the room.

It was *his* head that struck the wall. His hands clutched air. He fell head-long stunned, bleeding, and—presently, he was dead.

The room was very still. Awesomely silent.

Margaret Joyce was *in the air*, with her Lord!

CHAPTER XXVI.

A CASTAWAY.

MADGE and her husband left Albany on the Monday morning, ostensibly for a brief honey-moon, but, chiefly, with a view to recruit her husband's health. They had gone to a tiny little house among the Catskills, kept by a coloured woman named "Julie." The pastor had been there before, and had himself chosen this quiet retreat for their marriage trip.

The heart of Madge was broken, for her husband would not be friendly with her. He was barely civil when he spoke to her, and answered her in short, sharp monosyllables only. All the old natural pride, with which she would have met this treatment a fortnight ago, or less, was, fortunately, for *him*, swallowed up in her new found faith *in*, and her utter surrender *to* God. And with this there had come to her the patience and purifying, born of the Hope of the near return of the Lord, whom she now loved.

She had been alone, thinking over the whole position, for a couple of hours. The situation had become intolerable. She determined to make an appeal to him, though it hurt her natural pride even to contemplate it.

"Help me! Teach me! Guide me!" she cried unto her God. And in the strength of the divine promises of upholding and guidance, she decided to go to her husband.

* * * * * * *

He was alone, with a book before him on the table. But he was not reading. He was not even thinking.

His mind was in a confused whirl, born of the inward rage of a much discomfited man. He had made a fool of himself, in public. He knew it, and he had been too proud to apologize. He had spurned and snubbed the woman, for whom he had professed to be dying of love, and who had made the greatest sacrifice any honest woman can make to man—since she had offered herself to him, in marriage.

He knew that, in the eyes of his wife, and in the eyes of the little world he had lived and laboured in, that he had lowered himself, had proved himself less than ordinarily human.

Some of his own recent platform and pulpit utterances, returned to his mind, and they stung him by their reproach. The very last sermon he had preached, before his breakdown of health, had had for its text, "To him that overcometh, will I give———."

In the course of his address he had alluded to the shame of some of life's failures, and had quoted William S. Walsh's "Ichabod."

Now, as he sat brooding over his own fall, the lines returned to him. They mocked him, gibed at him, becoming, to his brooding imagination, sentient things with laughing, mocking, sneering voices, that somehow contrived to fling back into his ears, the very tones of his own voice, as he had declaimed the verses from his platform, weeks ago:

> "Alas, for the lofty dreaming,
>   The longed-for high emprise,
> For the man whose outer seeming
>   His inner self belies!
>
> "I looked on the life before me
>   With purpose high and true,
> When the passions of youth surged o'er me,
>   And the world was strange and true.

"Where the hero-soul rejoices
  I would play the hero's part;
My ears were attuned to the voices
  That speak to the poet's heart.

"I would conquer a place in story,
  With a soul unsmirched by sin;
My heart should be crowned with glory
  My heart be pure within.

"*But the hour that should have crowned me,*
  Cast all high hope adown,
And the time of trial found me,
  A sinner, coward, clown."

The thought that many of those who heard him declaim those lines, would be now recalling them, and perhaps be applying them to himself, half maddened him. And it was at this worst of all moments for her mission of reconciliation, that Madge entered the room.

With a rare gentleness she began to plead with him, reminding him of all the passionate love he had expressed for her up to the very moment, almost, when they entered the church together for that Sunday morning service.

He answered her coldly, sullenly at first. Then he grew pettishly angry with her, and snapped sharply at her, contradicting her in nearly all she said:

"But, Homer," she pleaded again, and in the deep yearning heart to win him back to his old loving self, she knelt before him, and tried to take his hand.

With an angry exclamation, he rose sharply to his feet and thrust her away with his foot, as he cried:—

"I don't want you! You go your way, I'll go mine, and——"

He stopped suddenly. With a sharp cry of agony, he stretched his hands out into the empty space, where an instant before, she had knelt—for, in one flashing moment, she had disappeared from before his eyes.

"Madge! Madge, dear love, dear love, dear wife!" he cried.

The sound of his own voice struck chilly upon his soul. Deep, deep down in his heart he knew what had happened—*only he would not own it to himself.*

He flashed a swift glance at the window and door. Both were fast shut.

"This is what Doig preached! What Madge believed would come to pass!" he cried, hoarsely.

There was a strange look of terror in his eyes.

"Julie will have gone, too, if it *is* the—the—."

He did not finish his muttered thought. Like a man walking in his sleep, he moved to the door, opened it and called, loudly:—"Julie!"

There came no reply. An eerie stillness was in the house.

He moved on into the kitchen, the room was empty. A saucepan of milk was boiling over on the hot-plate of the grate!

He hurried into the garden, calling "Madge! Julie!" There was no response.

He went back to the house. The turkeys had strayed into the kitchen, there being no one to drive them back. He made a hurried, fearsome tour of the house. Every room was empty!

He went back to where he had been, when Madge was taken, with a groan he dropped into his chair, staring into space with horror-stricken eyes.

Suddenly, as though a living voice utered them, the words of scripture sounded in his ears.

"Lest, that by any means, when I have preached to others, I myself should be a castaway."

A mortal agony filled his eyes, as he groaned:—

"God help me! I know now that I have only been a *minister*, by training and by profession, I have never been a son of God by conversion, by the New Birth!"

His untaught soul had misinterpreted the real inwardness of that passage of Paul's. But it was true, in the sense *he* meant it, he *was* "a castaway."

CHAPTER XXVII.

A STRICKEN CITY.

IT was not really until business time next morning, that London, that the whole country, really fully awoke to the fact of the great event of the previous night. Suburbans, in many cases, only heard the strange news on their arrival at their particular railway stations. Even then, a hundred rumours were the order of the moment. Everything reported was vague and shadowy. There were a few rank unbelievers of the garbled stories of the translation, who laughed sceptically, then began to grumble at the strange disorganization of the Railway traffic.

More than one annoyed, belated traveller, remarked in similar terms to the utterance of a commercial traveller, at Surbiton station:—

"If there is *any* actual truth in this story of the secret translation of a number of religious people, then the mysterious taking away of so many signal-men, and engine-men, will be an eye-opener to the travelling public, who never, somehow, suppose that Christianity is a strong factor in the lives of railway men."

"It is a revelation in another way," remarked a second, "since it suggests *why* we have hitherto had so few railway accidents, *compared with other nations.*"

The tens and hundreds of thousands, the millions, poured into London as usual. But the snap had gone out of most of them. A horrible sense of foreboding, was upon the spirits of the travellers. As the newspapers more fully confirmed the news, London approached perilously near the verge of a general panic.

The newspapers were bought up with phenominal eagerness. "Souf Efriken War worn't in it, fur clearin' out peepers!" a street seller remarked.

But few of the morning papers, (except the "Courier") had anything special to say on the great event. Most of them, in fact, were absolutely silent.

There were weather prophecies, political prophecies, financial prophecies, social prophecies, sporting prophecies, commercial prophecies,—but no prophecy of the Coming of the Christ.

The "Courier's" rival had a brief note to the effect:—

"Some wild, senseless rumours were abroad in London last night, as to the sudden, mysterious disappearance of numbers of the *ultra* religious persons of London, and elsewhere. Some people talked wildly of the end of the world. We therefore despatched special commissioners, to ascertain what truth there was in all this.

"Our representative returned an hour and a half later, after having visited all the chief places of amusement and principal restaurants. But everywhere managers told the same story, 'there has been no signs of the end of the world in *our* place. We are fuller than ever.'

"The genial manager of the ——— Theatre, assured our Representative, that no later than last Sunday morning, he heard it repeated at his Church, that 'as it was in the beginning, is now, and ever shall be, *world without end*, Amen.' So that, for the life of him, he could not conceive any one being such a fool as to talk of the *end* of the world."

But the note of the "Courier's" clarion call had no uncertain sound. Besides all that we have already seen written in the office by the translated Tom Hammond, and afterwards by Ralph Bastin, the latter had added to his postscript, another. It was a solemn, a pathetic word, and ran as follows:

"Our sheets must go to press in a few moments, if the "Courier" is to be in the hands of its readers at the usual hour. But before we print, we feel compelled to add a word or two more to what we wrote two hours ago.

"During the last two hours, we have made many discoveries, not the least of which, from the *personal* standpoint, is the fact, that the nearest and dearest being to our own heart and life, one whose life and thought, of late, has been strangely taken up by the Christ of God, is missing. She has shared in the glory and joy of the wondrous, mysterious, and—to *most* of us, to *all* of us surely who are *left*—*unexpected* translation.

"We have no wish or intention to parade our own personal griefs before our readers, but dare to say that no journalist ever worked with a more broken, crushed sense of life, than did we during the two hours we afterwards spent in searching London for facts.

"One curious fact which we speedily discovered, was, that no one had been taken in this wondrous translation, from any of the Theatres or music-halls. In the old days—four *hours* ago, seems, to look back to, like four centuries—before this awfully solemn event, discussions arose, periodically, in certain religious and semi-religious journals, as to whether *true* Christians could attend the theatre and music-hall.

"The fact that no one appears to have been translated from any of these London houses of amusement, answers, we think, that question, as it has never been answered before."

Here followed a brief *resume* of his experiences in other quarters. Then in big black type he asked the question:—

"WHAT FOLLOWS, (ACCORDING TO THE BIBLE PROGRAM) THIS STUPENDOUS EVENT?—The Bible, evidently, (when read aright) told those, who have been taken from our midst, that this translation was approaching, then it must surely give some hint of what we may expect to follow so startling an episode as that of to-night. The question is, *what* follows?

"There must surely be many clergymen and ministers who knew *about* this great translation, who though not living in the spirit of what they knew, and being therefore left behind, like the common ruck of those of us, who were carelessly ignorant—there must be many such ministers left, who could teach us *now, what* to expect *next,* and *how* to prepare for the next eruption—whatever form it may take.

"We therefore propose to any such ministers, that they gather us into the Albert Hall, Agricultural Hall, St. Paul's Cathedral, Spurgeon's Tabernacle, Whitfields —why not, in fact, into every church, chapel, Salvation Army Barracks, or even in the great open spaces such as Hyde Park, and other Parks, Primrose Hill, Hampstead Heath, etc., and teach us, who are left behind from the wondrous Translation, that has just occurred, how to be prepared for the next mighty change, for we believe the bulk of us are absolutely in the dark.

"Meanwhile, are there no houses in Paternoster Row, and its neighbourhood, where books and pamphlets on these momentous subjects can be obtained, or are all such publishers translated with those of whom we have been writing?"

One effect of the last suggestion, in Bastin's *second* postscript, was to send thousands of people to Paternoster Row, the Square, Ivy Lane, and all the neighbourhood. Some of the publishers of books on the Lord's Second Coming, *had* been *left* behind, had *not* shared in the Rapture of which they had printed and published.

Storekeepers, packers, masters, clerks, were most of them reading up the contents of their own wares. Business system among them, at first, seemed an unknown quantity. Deadness, amaze, fear, uncertainty, all of these things held and dominated them.

But they had to wake up. Their counters were besieged. Hordes of people thronged the doors. In twenty minutes after the first great influx, there was not a tract, a booklet, or a volume, on the "Lord's coming, and the events to follow," left in the "Row."

At any other time those in command of the stores, would have tried to get the printing presses at work, to run off some hundreds of thousands of the briefest of the "Second Advent" literature. But, to-day, fear, nameless fear held every one in thrall.

The "Row" put up shutters, and went home—or at least got away from business.

Business, everywhere, was at a standstill. By eleven o'clock most of the city houses were closed. Some of the banks never opened at all. Throgmorton Street and the Stock Exchange were in a state of dazed incredulity. A few members were missing, and these were known to be "Expectants" of the Translation.

"Salvation S——, is gone!" some one called out.

"Aye!" cried another, "I'd give all I possess, or ever hoped to possess, to be where he is now. I remember how he tried and prayed to persuade me once to——"

There was a rush of members across "The Floor" at that moment. Some one had a proposition to make, namely a trip to 101 Queen Victoria Street, to see if there were any Salvationists left there. A little band, about a dozen, responded, and the silk-hatted, excited little crowd swept away on their curious quest.

CHAPTER XXVIII.

"HALLELUJAH LASS."

THERE was one "Hallelujah Lass," in the front shop, at the "Headquarters." She was bonnetless, but the big, navy-blue head-dress laid on a glass show-case. She wore a finely-knitted crimson jersey and braided blue skirt. Her eyes were red with weeping. She was strangely distraught. There was no lilt of the song upon her lips :—

> "Oh! the peace my Saviour gives,
> Peace I never knew before."

"Not all translated then?" began the leader of the Stock Exchange band, addressing her.

There was nothing flippant, nothing sneering in his tone or manner.

The girl essayed a reply, but at first it ended in a sob only. Presently she recovered herself enough to say :—

"No, we're not *all* translated! You see, sir, the Army, as a body, never quite admitted the truth of *this* Second coming of our Lord. It has always preached that we, as an Army of Salvation, were raised up by God to get *all the world* converted. A lady in the train, as I came up to business, only yesterday——"

The girl sighed wearily, as she interpolated, "Yesterday seems as far off as Wesley's times. But, only yesterday, this lady, in the train talked to me about the 'Lord's near return'—that is how *she* put it—and said, 'God is undoubtedly using the Army in evangelizing the

distant heathen, and thus allowing them to fulfil His purpose in calling out those who are to form the Bride of
the Heavenly Bridegroom—but, believe me, my dear, the
world will never be converted *before* Christ comes for
His Church.'

"She talked to me very beautifully, and simply, only,
as she said, one could only grasp these truths in proportion as one kept clear in their minds the things which
belonged to the separate dispensations.

" 'If,' she said, 'The Lord came to-night'—how little
she or I dreamed that He actually would—'this dispen-
sation would be closed, and a new one would begin
to-morrow.' "

The girl looked around in a bewildered way, almost
as though she was looking for something she had lost.

"I have never known anything about the dispensations, and their bearing on the Bible," she went on. "The
Army has always taught us that we should *all* die, lie in
our graves until "the *last Day*," then appear before the
Great White Throne, and be judged according to our
lives, and all that. The lady who spoke to me yesterday
—yesterday? oh, how far off it seems—explained to me,
from the Bible, that true Christians would *never* appear
before the Great White Throne.

"That when the Great White Throne shall be set, the
real Christian will be seated in glory *with* Jesus, the
Judge. And only the wicked, unsaved dead will be judged
there. The sin of the *true* Christian, she said, is done
with, settled, put away at the Cross.

" 'There is therefore *now no* condemnation (*judgment*)
to them who are *in* Christ Jesus.' 'He that heareth, and
believeth on Jesus, *hath* everlasting life, and *shall not*

come into the judgment, but *is* passed from death unto life.'

"She told me that the true Christian, who might be living, when the Lord should Return, would be caught up *into the air,* with all the Christian dead, who will rise from their graves; and, that then the only judgment that can ever come to the Christian, will take place. That will be at Christ's judgment *of Rewards.* She said that eternal life did not enter into the question. That was settled once and for ever, but at Christ's Reward-judgment the Christian's *work* would be tried."

Some of the silk-hatted listening men began to fidget All this talk was foreign and uninteresting to them.

"The lady," the girl went on, "promised to meet me this morning at the station, at the same time as we met yesterday, *'Should the Lord Tarry'* she said. But I saw nothing of her this morning. She had been *'caught up,'* of course, to meet her Lord in the air, and I——"

The girl's voice broke, her eyes streamed with tears One of the youngest of the stock-brokers asked:—

"But why, if Salvationists are Christians, are *you* here Why were *you* not translated?"

"God help me!" she cried, "I know *now,* now that it is too late, that I was never converted. I was drawn into an Army meeting by reports I heard of the singing and music. The Army's methods fascinated me—the young officer who came to our town, was a very taking fellow. He talked to me in an after meeting, I wept with the many emotions that were at work within me I went to the penitent form—and—and—afterwards joined the Salvation Army—but I know *now,* I was not really saved."

She caught her breath in a quick sob, then a little glow suddenly filled her face, as she added:—

"But I have settled the matter this morning. I have yielded, intelligently to Christ, and I know that

> "Jesus with me is united,
>   Doubting and fears they are gone;
> With Him now my soul is delighted,
>   I and King Jesus are one."

"And," she cried, her eyes flashing with a holy light, "If witnessing for Jesus means martyrdom, then, by God's grace, I'll show by my death that——"

"Are there many Salvationists left?" interrupted one of her listeners.

A quick flush dyed her cheek; as she replied:—

"I *can't* say! There are some here at head-quarters, whom I should not have thought would have been *left behind*, but who are. Though I don't believe there will be more, if so many Salvationists, as other sects, *in proportion*, be found to be left behind, or——"

The sound of thousands of tramping feet broke into the girl's speech. The little crowd of Stock-brokers rushed to the door.

A dense mass of men and women were marching up the street. Every face was set and serious. There were many clergymen and ministers in the crowd, if the clerical collar and ministerial garb gave true indication of their calling.

"To St. Paul's! To St. Paul's!" a stentorian voice was shouting.

The stockbrokers joined the mighty crowd, which, grim, resolute, silent, swept on.

*   *   *   *   *   *   *

By midnight, or soon after, a few hours only after the great Translation, the hordes of the vicious that

festered in the slums—women, as well as men, *aliens* an
British alike—had heard something of what had hap
pened, and creeping from their filthy lairs, began, a
once to become a menace to public life and property.

Many of the police beats were unprotected, the me
who had been patrolling them sharing in the sudde
glorious Rapture of their Lord's return. By midnigh
the whole police service had become temporarily diso
ganized, if not actually demoralized.

Scotland Yard heads of departments were missing, a
well as local Superintendents, Sergeants, etc. In man
cases there was no one to give orders, or to maintai
control. And where leaders *were* left, they were ofte
too scared and unnerved to exercise a healthful authorit

Under these circumstances the hordes of vicious, an
out of work grew bolder every hour. They had no fea
of the Spiritual character of the strange situation, fc
God, to them, was a name only to blaspheme. Hell wa
a merry jest to them, a synonym for warmth and rest,—
a combination which had been all too rare with them o
earth. Besides, Hell had no shadow of terror to peopl
who, for years, had suffered the torments of a life in
literal hell in London.

Shops, and private houses, and some of the large
business houses had been openly burgled. A rumour gc
abroad, that the Banks were to be raided.

Ralph Bastin, passing the Bank of England, foun
that the guard of Soldiers had been quadrupled, and th
too for the *day*-time. Curious to know how the Transl
tion of the night before had affected the army, he aske
one of the privates if any of the London soldiers wei
missing?

"All the 'blue-lights,' (as we calls the Christians, sir,

is missin'. Yer see, sir, if a feller perfesses to be a Chrishun in the Army, an, aint real, 'e soon gits the perfession knocked outer 'im. On the other han' if 'e's real, why all the persekushun on'y drives 'is 'ligion deeper inter 'im. Yes, all the 'blue-lights' is gone, sir, an' any amount o' officers.

"These, as is gone, is mos'ly the middle-age an' ole ones, an' those wot's been in India, Malta, an' other furrin stations. I've knowed lots o' that sort o' officer, as oosed to hev Bible-Readin's at their Bungalows. Ah, they wur *right,* they wur, the other wur wrong, an' the wrong 'uns knows to-day as they's out o' luck!"

"If yer arsks my erpinun, ser, I sez, that London's full o' fools, to-day, fur if we'd all been doin' an' thinkin' as we'd oughter, why we'd be now up in Glory wi Jesus. I've yeard the truth at So'dger Homes, an' sich places, an' I've sung wi' lots o' others:—

> "Blessed are those whom the Lord finds watching;
>   In his glory they shall share:
> If He shall come at the dawn or midnight,
>   Will He find us watching there?"

> "O, can we say we are ready, brother?—
>   Ready for the soul's bright home?
> Say, will He find you and me still watching,
>   Waiting, waiting, when the Lord shall come?"

The man suddenly straightened himself, and glanced away from Bastin. An officer was approaching.

Ralph Bastin walked away, the thought that filled his mind, was of the strange mood that had suddenly come over *every*one, since to-day, everybody seemed ready to talk freely of religious things.

He moved on up Cheapside, his destination being St. Paul's Cathedral.

CHAPTER XXIX.

IN ST. PAUL'S.

THE cathedral was packed, packed out to the doors. The aisles, and every other inch of standing-room was a solid Jam. The whole area of the interior showed one black mass of silent waiting, expectant people—it was curious to note that almost every woman had donned black, in some form or other.

The great organ was silent. No one dreamed of singing. The choir seats were full of strangers. The stalls were filled with an indiscriminate crowd. There was no rule, no discipline to-day.

Suddenly the tall, square-built form of a certain well-known Bishop, rose near the pulpit. He had linked his arm in that of one of London's most popular Nonconformist preachers, and almost dragged him to his feet.

There was evidently a controversy going on between the two men as to which of them should address the people, each urging the other to lead off. The same thought was in the minds of nearly all who were in view of the pair, *namely,* "how comes it that a Bishop, and a popular preacher like the Rev. ——, have been left behind?"

A strange new tenseness, a deepening silence, settled upon the mighty mass gathered under that great dome. Suddenly the silence was broken by a voice calling:

"Bishop ——." Another voice immediately cried, "No! The Rev. ——."

A momentary clamour of voices ensued. The voices were not shrill in their eagerness, but sullen, sombre, almost savage, in fact. A moment, and the Bishop slowly entered the pulpit. He bowed his head in prayer.

Like the slow, rushing sound of the letting loose of some distant water, the noise of thousands of bending forms filled the place, for everyone bowed the head.

A moment later, the heads were raised. The silence almost of a tomb filled the place, when the first momentary rustle of the uprearing had subsided.

The voice of the Bishop broke the silence, crying:—

"Men and women of London, fellows with me in the greatest shame the world has ever known—the shame of bearing the name Christian, and yet of being the rejected of Christ,—we meet to-day under awful, solemn circumstances.

"We are face to face with the most solemnly awful situation the human race has ever known, if we except the conditions under which, during those three hours of blackness at Calvary, the people of Jerusalem were found, while the Crucified Christ hung mid-air, on the Fatal Tree.

"It may be said that our position bears some likeness to that of the people who were destroyed at the Flood. Those antedeluvians had one hundred and twenty years warning, we, as professing Christians, have had nearly two thousand years warning, yet, London, England and the whole world has by last night's events, been proved practically heathen—or atheist, atheist will perhaps best fit our character.

"The moment came when God called Noah and his family into the ark. But what never occurred to me, until this morning, was the significant fact, that God did not shut the door of the ark, or send the flood, until *seven days later,* thus giving the unbelievers another opportunity to be saved.

"And God has given London, England, America, the world, this same extra opportunity of being prepared for the Return of the Lord, and the Translation of His Church.

"For, for some years, now, conferences, and conventions, addresses, Bible-Readings, etc., where this subject of the Second Coming of Christ has been specially taught, has been multiplied mightily. I have been present at some of these gatherings, but, smiling amusedly at what I termed the wild utterances of visionaries, I neglected my opportunity.

"Yet, of all men, *I* ought to have been prepared for this Coming of the Lord. I have held ministerial office in a church that taught the doctrine, plainly, in many of its prayers and collects. But I see, now, that all through my life, I have been blinded by the *letter* of things, and have mistaken christening, confirmation, communicating, for conversion, and for life in Christ.

"I see, to-day, that I entered the established church of this realm, and not the family of God, and the service of Christ. I have never really been God's, by the New Birth, until last night, when my dear wife, in company with all the waiting, longing church, was suddenly called up to be with her Lord. Not by death, dear friends—she saw no death—but by that sudden translation, that has startled us all so."

A low sobbing sound ran through all the building. The gathered thousands, almost to a man, realised that they, with the speaker, were equally lifeless, spiritually.

"I was in the room when my wife disappeared," the

Bishop went on. "She had been very ill. It became necessary to perform a critical operation on her. I insisted on being present. I see the scene now.

"The nurses standing by the antiseptic baths with the sponges and clips immersed. In the eerie silence of that room, no sound came save the voice of the great surgeon, as he cried 'clip'—'iodoform'—'bandages.' Suddenly, as he half turned to take a bandage of the nurse, the form of my precious wife disappeared from the operating table. One of the nurses at the antiseptic bowl, was gone also.

"And I, a *professed* servant of the Christ who had called the translated ones, was *left,* with the great surgeon, and others, as you, dear friends, many, *most* perhaps, members of some Christian church, have been left.

"'Sister Carrie gone too!' cried the great surgeon, 'then you may depend, Bishop, that Christ has come for all His real church, for Nurse Carrie lived in daily, hourly expectation of some kind of translation.' With a puzzled look upon his face, he said, suddenly:

"'But, Bishop, how is it that you are left behind, who, of all men in our midst, one would have thought would have gone?'

"I had to say last night to him, dear friends, what, with shame and regret, I have to say to you now, that I *ought* to have known the Truth, and have been prepared, but because I was unconverted, I had failed to apprehend the fact of the Lord's near Return.

"Yet, how often, on the third Sunday in Advent, have I, with many of you, repeated the *Great Truth,* in the collect:—

"'O Lord Jesus Christ, who, at Thy first coming, didst send Thy messenger to prepare Thy way before Thee; Grant that the ministers and stewards of Thy mysteries, may likewise so prepare and make ready Thy way, by turning the hearts of the disobedient to the wisdom of the just, that at Thy *second* coming to judge the world, we may be found an acceptable people in Thy sight, who livest and reignest with the Father, and the Holy Spirit, ever one God, world without end. Amen.'

"In the burial of our dead, too, how often have I recited, and have heard the words,

" 'Beseeching Thee that it may please Thee, of Thy gracious goodness, *shortly to accomplish the number of Thine elect,* and to hasten Thy Kingdom; that we, *with* all those that are departed in the True faith of Thy Holy Name, may have our perfect consummation and bliss, both in body and soul, in Thy eternal and everlasting glory; through Jesus Christ our Lord.'

"Again, the words of Paul in the matter of the Lord's Supper 'TILL HE COME!' ought to have opened my eyes. But I confess, with shame, I have been blind, a blind leader of the blind ———"

Visible emotion checked the Bishop's speech, for a moment. Recovering himself, he went on:—

"A blind leader of the blind, because unborn of God. I *ought* to have known that Christ's Return was near. I *should* have known it, had I been spiritually-minded, by the signs of the Apostasy which, (prophesied to precede the Second Coming of the Lord) have been having their fulfilment all around us for years.

"Since last night, I have lived a whole life-time. I have read the whole of the Gospels and Epistles, and, taking my true place as a lost soul before God, I have been born of God. And now, here, in this solemn moment, I bring to you the Spirit-taught knowledge that has been given to me."

For a few minutes, he traversed ground already covered in these pages, then, continuing, he said:—

"Last Sunday, when, in all the pride of my office, I preached — preached in my unconscious unbelief — I quoted those lines of the poet:—

> "'They pass me like shadows, crowds on crowds,
>   Dim ghosts of men, that hover to and fro,
>   Hugging their bodies round them like their shrouds
>   Wherein their souls were buried long ago;
>   They trampled on their youth, and faith and love,
>   With Heaven's clear messages they madly strove,
>   And conquered—and their spirits turned to clay . . . .
>   Alas! poor fools, the anointed eye may trace
>   A dead soul's epitaph in every face.'

"To-day, friends, I know that 'the anointed eye' must have traced 'The dead soul's epitaph,' in my *life*, if not in my face.

"Now let us face our present position, as those who are *left!* What is the future to be? This is what you need to know, what I need to know! *First*, let me say, the next thing for each to do is to seek the Lord, to cry unto Him for mercy and pardon, while all our hearts are shocked and startled, and our thoughts are turned God-wards. For unless we close with God, become His, and live out the future to Him, our portion will be an Eternal Hell."

An awful hush rested upon the gathered thousands, as he proceeded:—

"One thing appears very plain from Scripture, that is, that when, last night, Christ came into the air and caught up His Church, living and dead, that the Devil, who has been the Prince of the Power of *the air*, had to descend to earth. Christ and Beelzebub can never live together in the same realm.

"In the re-creation of this earth, recorded in Genesis, God blessed everything that He created, *save the atmosphere*, He *did* not, He *could* not bless that because Satan, driven from the re-created earth, by the breath of the divine Spirit, had taken refuge *in the air*. He is therefore called in Scripture, not only the '*Prince of this World*,' but 'THE PRINCE OF THE POWER OF THE AIR.'

"Now, beloved, the Spirit of God has left the earth. The Devil has taken up his abode here with all his myriad agents, and he is going to make earth as hot for those of us who will witness for God, as is hell itself to the lost.

"If we will witness for God during the years we are beginning to-day—called the years of 'The Great Tribulation,' they will probably be seven in number, and extend therefore to the dawning moment of the Millenium—if we witness therefore for God, I say, during these intervening seven years, we may expect to meet with hideous trial and suffering.

"Antichrist will now soon make himself known—he will be a *man*, not a system, mind,—he will mislead the Jews, who will now, immediately, return to their own land, and build their New Temple. For a time, Antichrist will appear to be the friend of the Jews, but he will seek to force the most awful idolatry upon them. The mass of Jewry will accept all this.

"With the Jew, every Gentile will presently be compelled to accept Antichrist, and the Roman Beast——"

A sound of protest was heard from a seat near the pulpit, as the Bishop spoke of the "Roman Beast." But the preacher took no note of the interruption and went on:—

"The Devil will be so mad at being cast down out of

heaven, and because he knows such a very limited time to work against God, that he will call up all hell to stamp out God's people."

For one instant the Bishop paused. He leaned over the pulpit edge, his eyes were full of the light of a holy determination, but into his voice there crept a tender yearning, as he continued:—

"Are we prepared for actual martyrdom? For this will certainly be the fate of many who will not bear about upon them the mark of the Beast."

Again there came a growl from that seat near the pulpit. But the most solemn hush rested upon the vast mass of people.

CHAPTER XXX.

CONCLUSION.

QUIETLY, giving the impression that the sense of a great shame rested upon him, the Rev. —— —— the noted popular Nonconformist minister rose from his seat and faced the congregation.

Many of his own church were there. Many others, who had followed the criticisms of the more spiritual-toned Christian papers, upon his pulpit and other utterances, were there. Every one waited breathless, wondering what contribution he would make to the great matter in hand.

It was evident that it was only by the exercise of tremendous will-power that he could restrain his emotions sufficiently to speak.

"God help me, dear friends!" he began, "for I know now that I have been a Judas to the Lord of Life and Glory, whose *professed* servant I have been. I have gloried in my success; in the crowd that always filled my church; in the adulation of my intellectual powers by the Press. But I have never glorified Christ. In a hundred subtle ways I have denied my Lord —— He *is* my Lord *now*, I have found Him in the silence of the past awful night ——. I have been practically denying His deity for years, I have talked learnedly, when I ought to have been walking humbly, and—and——."

The strain was too much for him, tears streamed down his face, he covered his face with his hands, and dropped, sobbing, into his seat.

Sobs broke from many of the people. Weeping is infectious. In another moment the released pent-up emotions would have become a storm that none could have stayed. But the Bishop's voice called out,

"Let us pray!"

Every head was bent, and a prayer, such as London's Cathedral had never heard before, poured from the Bishop's lips. The conclusion of the prayer was followed by a moment or two of deepest stillness.

The silence was, suddenly, sharply broken by a full, rich voice crying:—

"Sit up, dear friends! Hear ye the word of the Lord!"

As the people lifted their heads a cry of amaze rang out from many throats:—

"The Monk of ———!"

The face of the Monk was familiar to all Londoners by his photograph, which beside being on sale in the shops, had appeared again and again in magazines. He had a striking figure, and there was a curious picturesqueness about his appearance, with his smooth, clean-shaven face, eagle eyes, tonsured crown, and curious purple-brown cowle'd habit, girdled with a stout yellow cord about the waist. His bare feet were sandaled. His hands, long, thin, with white tapering fingers, were outstretched a moment, then dropped slowly as he went on:—

"These are times when no one of us may shrink from speaking the truth boldly, if the Truth has been committed to us.

"With all due respect to our friend, Bishop ———, I would say, that all the surmises abroad in London, to-day, and those that have been voiced in our hearing here, during this hour, are wrong!

"The true meaning of the mysterious disappearance of

so many ultra-protestants, is this: The great end *is* near!
God's work was being frustrated by those unholy zealots,
who have been therefore graciously snatched away to hell,
before they could do further mischief.'

Murmurs of dissent and protest ran through the mass
of people, like the low sullen roar, at sea, of a coming
storm.

The Bishop thought of his Translated wife. He knew,
too, that God not only indwelt himself, now, but that
He had guided him in speaking to the people. He rose
in the pulpit to protest against the words of the Romanist.

But a voice cried out from the congregation:—

"Let the Monk have his say. These are strange times,
and we would hear all sides before we can judge."

And the Monk went on:—

"His supreme Holiness, the Pontiff, had been warned
of God—as he is God's Regent on earth—of the event
that has happened in our midst. His priests were warned
a few days ago, and in most of our churches, last Sunday,
certain dark hints of the coming catastrophe were given.
God therefore, now, calls upon you all, through me, to
turn to the *true* church, the *real* church, the church of
St. Peter's, the church of Rome ———."

A storm of protesting murmurs rolled up from the
people.

He waited, smiling confidently a moment. Then he
went on:

"When all the inhabitants of the earth bear upon them
the sign of the true church ———"

"THE MARK OF THE BEAST!" yelled a voice.

Another instant and there would have been a hideous
uproar, but that everything became forgotten in a new
excitement.

From outside, in the street, there rose the roar of a multitude, crying "Fire!" Fortunately the packed congregation within the Cathedral, one and all realised that the alarming thing was *out*side, not *in*side the building, so that there was no panic.

In a few minutes the great place was cleared. The Bishop, the Great Nonconformist, and a dozen other ministers, and laymen, remained gathered together as by a common instinct, by the pulpit.

"What is coming, brethren?"

"The *power* of Antichrist, and the manifestation of The man of Sin, himself," cried the Bishop, solemnly. "The Monk of ———," he went on "has been the first to voice the awful claims of this Man of Sin."

   *   *   *   *   *   *   *

   *   *   *   *   *   *   *

   *   *   *   *   *   *   *

A week later! ! !

Like a sow that returneth to the mire, London, England, the world had returned to its old careless life. The fever for sport, pleasure, money-getting, drinking, gambling, licentiousness, was fiercer than ever. Everyone aimed at forgetting what had happened a week before—and the bulk of the people were succeeding in finding the lethal element.

There had been many conversions during the first forty-eight hours *after* the Translation of the Church, but, since then, scarcely one. Already there had arisen, all over the land, all over the world in fact, as the American, Australasian, and Foreign Press Telegrams made clear, a multitude of men and women who were preaching the maddest, most dangerous doctrines.

Among the most popular, and successful, of these was

Spiritualism. Not the comparatively mild form known before the Great Translation, but an open, hideous blasphemous exhibition that proved itself to be, what it has really always been—*demonology*.

Antichrist's sway had begun. Satan was a *positive active*, agent. The restraints of the Holy Spirit were missing, for *HE* had left the earth when the Church had been taken away. Other restraints were also taken from the midst of the people, since, whether the world recognise it or not, the fact remains, that the people of God are the Salt, the preservative of the earth.

*　　*　　*　　*　　*　　*　　*

Final word! Whether or no, the writer has failed in the purpose he had when he set pen to paper; whether or no he has bungled his subject; whether the reader is or is not willing to accept the main statements of the special teaching in this book, does not really affect the real question, namely, *The Near Return of our Lord.* His word to us, whether we believe and accept it, or whether we slight and reject it, is:—

"BEHOLD I COME QUICKLY!" Be ye also ready, for in such an hour as ye think not, the Son of Man COMETH."

"For the Lord Himself SHALL descend from Heaven. * * * And the dead in Christ shall rise FIRST: Then, we which are alive and remain shall be Caught up together with them IN THE CLOUDS, to meet the Lord IN THE AIR: and so shall we ever be with the Lord!

TO - DAY ?

PERHAPS !

The continuation of this Book is published under the title "The Mark of the Beast."

INSPIRATIONAL TRUE STORIES
OF COURAGE AND FAITH
Complete and Unabridged

ORDER FROM YOUR BOOKSTORE

MORE CHALLENGING READING
FROM YOUR FAVORITE AUTHORS
Complete and Unabridged

GOD'S PSYCHIATRY by Charles L. Allen   75¢
An actual working manual which can change your life in just seven days. From Biblical lessons come ways to banish fear, acquire confidence, and face life with new enthusiasm and peace of mind.

THE BURDEN IS LIGHT! by Eugenia Price   75¢
The amazing autobiography of a successful, sophisticated writer whose empty personal life was transformed when she took the Word of God literally!

A MAN CALLED PETER by Catherine Marshall   1.25
The glowing story of the acclaimed minister and Senate chaplain whose messages touched the heartstrings of the whole world.

PEACE WITH GOD by Billy Graham   95¢
Written by one of the century's most influential religious figures, here is inspiration and comfort for the man in the street.

ANGEL UNAWARE by Dale Evans Rogers   60¢
The poignant story of the birth, and death, of Roy and Dale Rogers' own little girl. A lasting victory over great sorrow.

THROUGH GATES OF SPLENDOR by Elisabeth Elliot   95¢
An on-the-scene account of the martyrdom of five American missionaries in the steaming jungles of Ecuador, an epic of unmatched courage and faith.

THE LITTLE PEOPLE by David Wilkerson   75¢
Conceived in hate, born without love, robbed of their childhood — these are the children of addicts and prostitutes, muggers and alcoholics. Here is their story, who they are, how they exist, and what happens to them.